The *Chaplin Cane*

A Novel

Written by Carl Mendelsohn

Suite 300 - 990 Fort St
Victoria, BC, Canada, V8V 3K2
www.friesenpress.com

Copyright © 2015 by Carl Mendelsohn
First Edition — 2015

All rights reserved.

Editor: Eva Almos

No part of this publication may be reproduced in any form, or by any means, electronic or mechanical, including photocopying, recording, or any information browsing, storage, or retrieval system, without permission in writing from FriesenPress.

ISBN
978-1-4602-7783-6 (Hardcover)
978-1-4602-7784-3 (Paperback)
978-1-4602-7785-0 (eBook)

1. Fiction, Humorous

Distributed to the trade by The Ingram Book Company

ACKNOWLEDGMENTS

For:

My four Muses:

Ruth

Rose

Luisa

And

Eva

CHAPTER I

In the month of November 1949, on the cusp of the Scorpio, Calman Mencher decided that it was time for a reckoning. It was now twenty-eight years since he had made his debut on Planet Earth, red and raw and raging, until someone slapped his bottom and set him straight.

The day also marked three weeks since Calman had cleared his desk, resigned his job, and stormed out of Vince Saunders' office, where he had articled as an accounting student until his graduation only a year before. And it was also the day Calman, or Cal, as his friends called him, opened an office to practice his profession of public accountancy. Yes, it was time for a reckoning. Now, as he sat in his newly-acquired swivel chair, gazing out of the window, he wondered if Bennit had not been right.

Bennit Moranz had been in the same graduating class as Calman, and they had become friends. However, they had little in common, except for their love of tennis. That was how they had met – at the Huron Tennis Club, now extinct.

Bennit was conservative in his values as well as in his attitudes. Except for the tennis court, Bennit was never to be seen without a white shirt, and black or navy tie, and double-breasted jacket. His reddish-blond, wavy hair was always neatly coiffed.

Calman, on the other hand, was anti-tradition. He only wore a suit on state occasions – weddings and funerals. Otherwise he was to be observed wearing slacks, a sports jacket and open-necked shirt.

Bennit always played it safe. He never wagered, not even on the outcome of a tennis match. And he was insistent that his friends call him Bennit and not Ben, and especially not Benny. Calman liked his friends to call him 'Cal', and he was thinking of changing his name legally to Cal.

"Cal," Bennit had cautioned him, "I think you're making a mistake to be renting an office so soon after graduating. After all, you only have a few clients, and you'll barely make enough to cover your expenses."

"I hear you," Calman said, "but I believe it's time for me to cross the Rubicon."

"Oh, yes, Caesar, and what is that supposed to mean?"

"Well, there comes a time when one's destiny is challenged, and a guy has to take a risk. I think that the time is now ripe for me."

"Cal," the pragmatic Bennit replied. "I know you're a great reader, but when did you switch from poetry and novels to science fiction? You're being irrational, you know. This notion of starting an office now is one of your flights of fancy."

"Bennit, I appreciate your advice, but in case of fact, you're in the same position as me. Right now you're working from the kitchen table in your parent's home. Very soon, you too will have to launch out. So I'll make you a proposition. Let's form a partnership. Then we could share costs, and reduce our exposure. What do you say?"

"Well!" Bennit demurred. "Do you mean an equal partnership? I suspect that your gross income is greater than mine."

Calman had not given any thought to a partnership with Bennit. The words had just blurted out, but having said them, he plunged ahead.

"Yes, that's exactly what I mean. You know there are a lot of advantages to a partnership…"

Bennit cut him off. "No! I'm not ready for that yet. I think I'll just continue to operate from my home."

"Bennit," Calman tried once more. "What are you fearful of? Life is full of chances. Every time you cross the street, you take the chance you won't be hit by a car; and every time you eat chicken you take the chance you won't choke on a bone…"

"Yeah! I know!" Bennit said, cynically. "And every time you get laid you take a chance you won't come down with a case of the clap."

"Speak for yourself!" Calman said wryly.

After a few moments of strained silence, Bennit said in a conciliatory voice, "I know a couple of guys who have some extra space they would be willing to lease to you. You could get a package deal, which would include a receptionist, a typist and a small private office. Would you like me to contact them?"

Calman was hesitant, and then he exhaled wearily, lazily. "Maybe! I guess it can't hurt."

A few days later Calman was having dinner at home when the phone rang. His mother, a short, plump little woman, who had brought with her from London's Piccadilly Square a soprano voice and a Cockney accent, answered it.

"It's for you Cal," she said. "Be quick, your supper's getting cold."

"Hello! Is this Calman Mencher?" The voice on the phone was male and friendly.

"Yes! This is he," Calman replied.

"This is Charlie Tepper. I understand you want to lease some office space."

Calman was taken aback. He had not expected Bennit to act so quickly. The name Charlie Tepper sounded familiar, but he could not recall where he had heard it.

"Well," he mumbled, "I'm afraid I can't afford to pay much."

"Don't worry about that," Tepper interrupted him. "Come up to my office tomorrow and we'll make a deal."

The following day Calman appeared at Tepper's office, which was located on Bathurst Street, just south of Bloor Street, in central Toronto. The large store window, on the ground floor of the two-storey building, displayed in large black print the words "Charles H. Tepper, barrister and solicitor." A light went on in Calman's mind. Of course, he had heard of Charles Tepper. He was the lawyer who had incorporated his client, Ideal Upholstery, which was located down the street from Charlie's office.

Calman opened the door, and entered the vestibule of Tepper's law office. He was struck at once with the utter chaos that greeted him – pandemonium everywhere. The office area was a large square, divided into twelve cubicles, each containing a small desk and chair, and a four-drawer filing cabinet, cluttered with files. A clerk was walking rapidly across the room carrying a half-filled cup of coffee in one hand, two or three files in the other; a cigarette dangled from her mouth. She disappeared into a private office. Another woman clerk sat at her desk sifting and sorting papers.

"Yah!" she spoke loudly into a phone, which was cocked, against her ear. "That's what I said! Come in at two o'clock to sign the papers. Closing will probably take place tomorrow."

Two young female stenos were typing away in staccato, *clickety-clack*, *clickety-clack*, one with a cigarette in her mouth, the other pausing now and then to sip from her coffee cup. An articling student was poring over some documents, underlining important paragraphs, and taking large bites out of his sandwich. And two clients were wandering about, waiting for someone to call "next".

Calman looked about, trying to get someone's attention, when he noticed a young woman sitting behind a glass partition with a circular hole, which had been cut into its centre. Her feet were raised on a stool, and she sat back filing her fingernails. He figured that she must be the receptionist, so he approached her. She looked up at him, without losing the rhythm of her filing. Suddenly, a screeching wail assailed his ears.

"What in the world is that?" he asked the girl behind the glass partition.

"Oh!" she said, matter-of-factly. "That's just Charlie Tepper in his office practicing on his violin."

"A regular Paganini," Calman mused aloud, with a touch of sarcasm accentuating his voice. She laughed.

He continued, "Would you please inform Mr. Paganini that Mr. Calman Mencher is here for his appointment?"

She swung her feet off the stool and stood up, examined her fingernails, and walked towards an office from whence the squeaking was emanating.

"Hey! Paganini!" she yelled, reveling in the new appellation of her boss. "A Mr. Calman Mencher says he has an appointment with you. Should I send him in?"

Something was said from within, and she motioned Calman into the office. Charlie was placing his violin on top of a disorganized pile of letters and documents strewn over his desk. He deposited the bow gingerly in the wastebasket, and then turned to face Calman; he was all smiles, his hand outstretched in greeting. Calman took an immediate liking to this man who stood almost six foot two, and nearly a head taller than himself. Charlie had bushy eyebrows, and a curly head of black hair, which was somewhat disheveled; it was beginning to grey at the temples, and framed his oblong face. His trousers were baggy, and his jacket hung loosely. He appeared not to have a worry in the world.

Charlie was the first one to speak, "Do you play an instrument?"

"The best I can muster is 'chopsticks' with two fingers, on the piano," Cal said.

"That's too bad. I hoped you played the fiddle." Calman smiled, and Charlie shifted the subject matter.

"So I hear you want to rent some space from me."

Calman stopped him. "Now that's odd! My understanding was that you wanted to lease space to *me*."

"OK," said the affable Charlie, "Here's why I called you. Your client, Abe Schnier, came to see me last week, and asked me, as a favour to him, to find some space for you so that you could be near to him."

"Now that is really bizarre. Abe never mentioned it to me. My friend, Bennit Moranz, told me about the space."

"Who's this Bennit?" asked Charlie. "Oh, just a minute. You mean Benny."

"You'll make a life-time enemy if you call him Benny. Anyhow what kind of space do you have, and what will the rent be?"

"I happen to have a vacant apartment above my office," said Charlie. "There's a separate set of stairs leading up to it with direct access to the street. You can have it for fifty bucks a month."

"Is that gross or net?"

"That will be net. No! Gross!" Charlie laughed. "OK. We'll make it Gross."

"May I take a look at the space?"

"Yes, of course! Here are the keys." He handed Calman a set of keys. Calman ascended the stairs, and entered the suite. He inspected the rooms and then returned to Charlie's office.

"Charlie," he said, "To tell you the truth, it needs a lot of work. I'll give you forty bucks."

Charlie's laugh was infectious, "Make it forty-five."

"It's a deal!" They shook hands. "

I'll prepare a lease," said Charlie. "It'll be ready tomorrow. You can drop in any time. Let me see, do you spell your name with an 'a' or an 'e'?"

Calman spelled out his name slowly as Charlie printed it out. Then, as an afterthought, Calman asked him, "Say, by any chance, are you related to the Teppermans, the demolition people?"

"No! My name was actually 'Tupper', but I changed it to 'Tepper'." *Charles Tupper*, Calman thought. The name had a familiar ring.

"Wasn't Charles Tupper the name of one of the Fathers of Confederation?"

"He was my great-grandfather," Charlie chuckled.

Calman was enjoying the joke, and retorted: "Why did you want to change such a distinguished name to 'Tepper'?"

"It didn't sound Jewish enough." Charlie's secretary had entered the room and she caught their last exchange. "He's a regular comedian. He should be in vaudeville," she quipped. "The Arnolds are here. Shall I show them in?"

CHAPTER II

Calman was now situated in his new suites. He had borrowed a thousand dollars from his bank to paint the walls, sand the floors, and put up a plaque on the brick wall at the downstairs entranceway to his offices, but he still needed furniture – a desk, chairs, filing cabinets, which he could ill afford to buy. He began to wonder whether Bennit had not been right after all. Had he been too rash in taking the offices?

He was standing there, in the centre of his empty offices, puzzling over his predicament, when the phone rang. It was Angela, Abe's secretary.

"Hello, Calman?" she said, and without waiting for a reply. "Don't leave your offices; the furniture is on the way."

Abe Schnier, Calman's client, had come to the rescue. Abe was in the upholstery business, and his company was located just down the street from Charlie's offices. Abe had acquired a new secretary, the bosomy Angela Costello, who was willing to stay late and perform certain rites for Abe which his wife would not. Angela also took a kind of maternal interest in Calman.

One day Abe walked into his office to find all his old furniture piled into a corner, and new office furniture installed.

"There, now! Isn't that better?" Angela grinned. Abe scratched his head.

"How much did it cost?" he asked good-naturedly. Abe's discarded furniture wound up in Calman's office – desk, comfortable swivel chair, console, cabinets, waste baskets, even a typewriter – and now Calman was installed in his newly rented premises, ready to do business.

Calman cleared away the last file, rearranged a couple of chairs, found an appropriate spot on the wall to hang his degree, and sat down to relax in his newly acquired swivel chair. He filled his pipe with an aromatic tobacco and lit up. Leaning back in the chair, he began his reckoning.

What had he accomplished in these twenty-eight years? He had been born. The only mishap he had suffered was the time Aunt Kate, the family spinster, had been bouncing and tossing him about when he was an infant, and dropped him. He had landed on his head. *Dad never forgave her*, he thought as he extended his hand to his head, and felt around the pate, but found no unusual bumps. He was healthy and robust, and he played tennis. He had survived the Great Depression. And he had served during World War II. He had made it through university with a bachelor's degree in English, and then he had become a Chartered Accountant. Now he had started his own practice, and had even opened an office.

Now Calman's thoughts drifted to the day in the late fall of 1945. Vincent Saunders was going to interview him for a position as an articling student in his accounting firm. Calman had a head start against the other applicants because he had already completed two years of his accounting course prior to enlisting in the R.C.A.F.

The elevator rose to the fourteenth floor. Actually, it was the thirteenth floor, but many people were superstitious about the number thirteen, believing it brought bad luck, so almost every high rise skipped the number thirteen.

Calman turned the brass knob of the door at number 1401, and stepped into a small room. He immediately noticed the pretty girl sitting behind a partition. She was preoccupied, typing. He cleared his throat in an effort to attract her attention – "Ahem!" She looked up and smiled. He observed that when she smiled her whole face lit up, and even the room became illuminated. Her large dark eyes seemed to be dancing, and he also noted that her teeth were sparkling white. He was the first to speak.

"Good morning! I have an appointment with Mr. Saunders."

"You must be Mr. Calman Mencher."

He nodded.

"Please take a seat. He'll be with you shortly."

Calman took in the ambience in the reception room. It was small. He sat down in one of the two upholstered armchairs, and noted that it was comfortable. There was also a bench, which could hold two to three persons, comfortably, and a black console table on which several magazines were neatly arranged. Three framed black and white drawings adorned the walls, each depicting caricatures of gentlemen, in nineteenth century garb, in counting houses. Apart from these few items, the room was sparse. The young lady dialled someone, and spoke briefly into the phone. After returning the phone to its cradle, she stood up and walked towards Calman. She extended her hand, which he took.

"I'm Elsie. I'm the receptionist, typist and general gofer," she said."

He now noticed that she was very thin, which made her seem taller than her five feet five inches; she was also very pretty. A few minutes elapsed and then a door leading to the inner offices opened, and another lady entered, or rather bounded, into the room.

"Hello!" her cheerful voice rang out. "I'm Marie, Vince Saunders' secretary."

Calman took in this apparition. *Wow,* he thought. *She was certainly a statuesque beauty… very well endowed… spectacular.* Calman realized that he was ogling, and looked away in embarrassment. When he felt safe, he glanced at her again. He noted that she was slightly taller than him – about five foot nine. Her long black tresses shimmered, her black eyes flashed, and her voice rang as if in song. She led him to the door of Saunders's office, opened it, and ushered him in.

He found himself standing, rather ill at ease, raincoat draped over his right arm, in the 'sanctum sanctorum', as the staff referred to Saunders' office. Seated behind a large, red burnished mahogany desk, in a comfortable brown leather chair, talking on the telephone was the gentleman: the pretentious Vincent P. Saunders himself. He motioned to Calman to be seated, without raising his eyes from the paper on which he was doodling.

Calman sized him up. He was not tall, perhaps five foot six. Calman noticed that his fingers were long, and tapered. He could have been an artist, or a violinist. His fingernails were manicured and his hair was plentiful and well-coiffed. It seemed to Calman that it had been sculpted, and parted down the middle. He was also clean-shaven, and his cheeks bore the slightest tint of roseate—the first sign of high blood pressure, and an omen of the devastating stroke that would lay him low in years to come.

He wore a blue serge suit, and a matching tie, which contrasted with his white, crisp shirt. Calman sat down, and waited patiently for Saunders to finish his conversation. He also took note of the man's speech. Saunders was impeccably articulate, and affected a British accent. His speech, however, sounded counterfeit, the accent phony.

A few weeks later, Calman realized that Saunders had been talking to his wife, and he surmised she was probably saying to him, "Velvel, cut the bullshit. Who've you got there in your office that you're trying to impress?"

After about five minutes, which seemed to be interminable to Calman, the gentleman behind the desk restored the receiver and, sitting back, adjusted his glasses and pinched the bridge of his nose, an affectation he assumed when he was about to deliver a profound utterance.

"Let me see now…and you are?" but he was cut short by Calman's interruption.

"Calman Mencher, Sir. You were going to interview me for a position with your firm." Calman's voice had gone up a couple of octaves, revealing his nervousness.

"Oh, yes. You're the lad who wants to article with us as an accounting student."

The lad! The words shot through Calman's mind. *Why, this s.o.b! I served nearly four years with the R.C.A.F. Where was he during the war?*

But Calman needed the placement, so he choked out the words, "Yes, sir."

"Hmmm…" Saunders mused as he began to read Calman's résumé. After a few moments, with eyes still cast down on the paper, he remarked, "I see you're an 'A' student, and I see you'll be writing your finals in three years. That's good."

Calman's spirits began to rise. Perhaps he had misjudged the man. Saunders placed the paper on the desk, and straightened its creases. He was meticulous. Calman was learning his first lesson – never litter your desk. Then, drumming his fingers on the desk, he said, "I think we can find a place for you in our firm, Cal."

Wow! Calman uttered the expletive soundlessly. *He used my familiar name. I'm in!* He sat at the edge of the chair buoyed by expectancy. Saunders's fingers were interlaced, his elbows resting on the desk. Saunders would assume this posture whenever he was about to strike.

"You'll have to work hard," he said as Calman nodded vigorously, revealing his anxiousness once again. "You understand our modus operandi is quite different from that of other accounting firms. You will not be making green check marks for long. You'll be handling working papers, preparing schedules, and financial analyses. Within six months, I'll be expecting you to prepare financial statements. And by the end of the year, you'll be preparing tax returns. In your last year, I will expect you to be conferring with clients. All of this will take a lot of hard work, and a lot of application and responsibility."

He smiled his charming smile. "Think you can handle it?" Calman jumped up, but Saunders indicated he was to remain seated. Calman sat down quickly, eyes riveted on this accounting god.

Saunders pressed down on a button which was located at the edge of his desk, and spoke into an intercom.

"Marie, would you mind dropping in for a moment, please?" Calman immediately noticed that his voice had changed from an imperial tone to one of diffidence when addressing her.

Marie Dunn, who had shown Calman into Saunders' "chambers" twenty minutes earlier, came loping in, all smiles. Calman immediately stood up. She was a magnificent specimen of the female Homo sapiens. Calman's loins quivered. So did Vince's.

"This young man is joining our firm, Marie. His name is Calman, with a 'C', Mencher…"

"With an "M"? She added good-humouredly. Calman shook her proffered hand, smiling back at her.

"Order a briefcase for Calman, and have his initials engraved on it," Calman's new boss said.

"OK," said Marie and turned around to exit.

"Gold Leaf," Vince called after her. She gave Calman a cheerful look as she opened the door.

"I'll have it for you tomorrow," she said pleasantly.

Vince pointed to the chair again, and Calman sat down obediently, elated. Little did he realize that though Vince's tongue dripped manna, the serpent was about to strike.

"Now," Vincent said, "Let's talk salary." He was taking his time, fingering the papers on his desk, and talking slowly. "According to your résumé you have just been discharged from the Army."

"Air Force!" Calman corrected him, "In September."

"Right! And I believe you are entitled to a Veteran's allowance."

"A hundred dollars per month."

"Very well! Now, I'm sure you realize that we can't afford to pay very much to students. You're here to learn, not to earn," Vince smiled at his insipid attempt at humour. "You'll be making a sacrifice for the short run, but the reward will be great in the long run. I will be making an investment in you…and you will be making an investment in me. Do you follow me?"

Calman had no idea what he was leading up to, but he listened with trepidation.

"So-o-o…you will assign your Veteran's allowance to me. I will pay you twenty dollars per month until you graduate."

Calman was dumbstruck. Had he heard him correctly? Before Calman could reply, Saunders continued, "After graduation your monthly remuneration will increase to three hundred dollars," and as if to assuage his doubts, added, "And, of course, your name and designation will be included on the firm's letterhead."

Calman's knitted his brow, in consternation, and he averted his gaze. It seemed like a dream.

"One year after receiving your accounting designation you will become a junior partner of the firm, and at the end of two years, you will be elevated to senior partner."

Calman felt deflated as he tried to process all he had heard.

"A full partnership at the end of two years!" Saunders continued. "There you have it…a lick and a promise."

Calman returned to his earlier assessment of Vince Saunders: that he was a cheap s.o.b. But there wasn't much he could do; he needed to be articled in order to complete his studies. As he was hesitating, Vince started to give him sharp glances.

"That will be all," he announced summarily. Calman, dazed by the events that had just transpired, walked slowly towards the door.

CHAPTER III

Calman lifted the receiver and dialled his friend, Bennit Moranz. "Hello, Bennit? I called to remind you that I'll be picking you up tomorrow at seven a.m."

"Yes, I know!" Bennit replied, "We're going to Muskoka Lodge."

The two friends set out early Friday morning in Calman's new Vauxhall. Their mission was a girl-hunting expedition. They were a couple of lonely bachelors on the make. Muskoka Lodge was the market place where singles went to observe, and to be observed. The summer weather had lasted long into the fall, and the candidates would still be flocking to the lodge. As the pair wended their way north along Highway Eleven, nature revealed herself to them in a panorama of colours – red, green, ochre, yellow. Calman thought of the poet Shelley's Ode – "the leaves are yellow and black, and pale, and hectic red." Everywhere the foliage was rich and vivid and lush.

"Wow, Bennit! Look at that," said Calman, "It's like entering wonderland." Bennit snorted.

"What's so great about it? It's nothing new. It's the same as this each year."

"That's true! But the autumn colours somehow never cease to astonish me. Don't they give you a feeling of animation, like a sense of rebirth?

If I had the power, I would change the beginning of the New Year to the Autumnal Equinox. Don't you agree?"

"No," said the pragmatic and unimaginative Bennit, "I don't. You've been reading too much poetry in those English courses you take. Personally, I think that the white snow of January is far more in keeping with renewal."

Calman could not disagree with his logic. "The trouble with you, my friend," said Calman, "is that you've got no soul."

Bennit made no retort, and they drove on in silence. But Calman continued to marvel at the splendour of the woods on either side of the highway. After a while, Bennit broke the silence.

"Are you still looking for office space?"

"Thanks! I leased an office from Charlie Tepper."

"Ah, the lawyer!"

They had arrived at the Lodge just in time for lunch. After checking in, they entered the dining hall, only to find it nearly empty.

"I guess people will start arriving by evening," Bennit remarked with some disappointment. "What would you like to do?"

Calman thought for a moment.

"Well, the tennis courts are closed for the season, and it's too cold for a swim in the lake. I think I'll go to the room and read. What are you going to do?"

"I think I'll take a stroll and explore the grounds," Bennit said. "You never know who you might run into."

Two hours later Calman was still reading when Bennit sauntered into the room. "Any luck?" Calman asked.

"If you go fishing in the right places you're bound to catch something," Bennit answered.

"So, Mr. Piscator, what kind of fish is on the menu tonight?"

"A couple of minnows!" replied Bennit, with a self-satisfied look. "I ran into two sophomores, and we struck up a conversation. They're going to join us for dinner at seven-thirty."

"Sophomores! Wow! Did you know that could be jail bait?" Calman exclaimed. "Throw them back into the water."

"Too late, I've made the arrangements."

Calman and Bennit entered the dining room and were seated at a table overlooking the lake. Though it was too dark to see it, they could hear the waves breaking against the shore. After a short silence, Bennit remarked, "Well at least the setting is romantic."

Calman looked around and saw two young women being escorted toward their table.

"I think your two sophomores are here," he said. One of the girls was petite, pretty and dressed elegantly. Calman noted that her nose was like a button, and her eyes were slanted, almost Asian.

Then he speculated, "That must be where the expression, 'cute as a button', comes from." The other lady was taller, heavy and dowdy. He raised his eyebrows and gave Bennit a knowing look.

"Somehow I don't care for yours," Calman declared. "It's each man for himself," Bennit retorted. The men stood up to greet the ladies, and Bennit made the introductions.

"This is my friend, Cal Mencher. This is Evelyn Schwartz…" Calman shook hands with the pretty one, "and this is Sonia Krueger."

Bennit ordered a bottle of wine. The conversation started off at a slow pace – the usual getting-to-know-you talk… "Where do you live, what do you do, how long are you planning to stay?" The wine steward returned with the bottle, and poured a little into Bennit's glass.

Calman watched, in amusement, as Bennit, who rarely drank wine and whose experience in wine-tasting was limited to the Passover kosher syrupy stuff, inhaled the contents, then twirled the glass, as he had seen experts do. He finally drank it, rolling the contents around in his mouth before swallowing. He nodded to the steward nonchalantly: "It will do." The girls watched Bennit perform the rite with awe.

Calman saw that Bennit was rapidly winning points with the girls, so he said sarcastically, "Did you know that he's a wine connoisseur?"

The girls missed the irony, and instead of being deflated, Bennit rose in their esteem. Calman realized that he had to act quickly to minimize the damage.

"So Evelyn Schwartz," he began, addressing button-nose, "Do you know Izzie Schwartz? He manufactures ladies' coats. He's located on Spadina Avenue, at the corner of Richmond Street?"

"I should," she squealed. "He's my father."

Bennit caught the look of panic in Calman's eyes. Trying to hide his discomfort, and affecting a tone of good-natured geniality, Calman said, "Well, well! Isn't that a coincidence? Izzie is one of my clients."

At the same time, his tone rang out a message to Bennit.

Hands off!

Bennit got the hint, and the remainder of the evening was pleasantly dull.

The following day the weather had turned colder, and the two friends wore heavy sweatshirts as they breakfasted.

"It was a mistake for us to come here," Calman remarked, sipping his black coffee. "I didn't realize it would be so cold. Let's head for home after lunch."

"Frankly," Bennit sniffed. "I think you were thrown by finding yourself in a situation with your client's daughter. She put a crimp in your style. But she was kind of cute, and I was planning to make a play for her, myself. But I understand your dilemma. OK. I don't have much to pack. We can leave after breakfast."

The drive home was hopelessly silent. Two single guys, ripe for the plucking, were returning home, flummoxed…on their beams' ends. As if to compound their disappointment, Nature, that great magician, had performed a morphological disappearing act on them. Gone were the brilliant hues, transformed into pale yellows and browns. Gone was the verdant forest, leaving pines stripped naked – haunted, undernourished ghosts. Only the proud evergreens with their barren branches remained glistening with wintriness.

CHAPTER IV

Calman arrived at his office early on Monday morning, and ran into Charlie Tepper as he was about to enter his office. They greeted each other.

"Good morning Cal. Say, why don't join me for a coffee?"

Calman followed Charlie into his office, and Charlie's receptionist greeted them.

"Sally," said Charlie, smiling at her. "How would you like to go next door and bring back a couple of bagels?"

Charlie made a straight line to his private office, while Calman had to navigate his way through a path strewn with papers, files, ledgers, spit balls and other office debris. He shook his head in amazement as he took in the clutter – files strewn on the desk, on chairs, on the floor, some with documents tumbling out. A pipe lay on the desk with a tobacco pouch; half of the tobacco had spilled out, and was scattered amongst the files.

In one corner of Charlie's office, Calman noticed an old brass umbrella holder containing a staff. Calman picked it up and started examining it. The stick felt good to the touch. The shaft was long, with a shiny, black, smooth surface, except for the upper part, which was a mustard colour and had been peppered with little holes, providing a rougher surface for gripping. The top of the handle was shaped into a knob, and it seemed to

Calman that it had the appearance of an unfinished face. On the very top, or head, was mounted a silver disk embedded with turquoise stones.

Charlie made himself comfortable and motioned to Calman to do likewise, which Calman immediately did by sitting down, and raising his feet onto a corner of an ottoman, located adjacent to the chair, and crossing his ankles. He felt at ease with Charlie.

Calman held onto the staff and asked Charlie, "Where did you get this pole?"

"I don't know," Charlie, replied, "I guess somebody must have left it here."

The girl brought in the bagels, and two cups of coffee. Pointing to a black violin case propped up against a cabinet, Calman asked, "Is there a violin in that case?"

"Oh! Yeah. That's my violin. I'll take it home today. The boys are coming up this evening. We have a regular weekly quartet at my home. Do you play?"

"No, but I wish I did," Calman said. "Who do you play with, and what pieces do you play?"

"Oh! I've got a few buddies who are the regulars, and then we have a cellist, a flutist and a clarinetist who show up once in a while. We play mostly classical… You know… Handel, Mozart, Haydn, Mendelssohn, and Beethoven. We have a lot of fun. Every now and then guys from the Toronto Symphony join us. Afterwards we have coffee and watch porno films."

"What? Did you say 'porno films'? Now you're kidding me, aren't you?"

"No! I'll invite you up the next time we have a music session at my place"

"Wow!" Calman exclaimed. "What a great combination – symphony and pornography. Have you ever thought of patenting the idea?" Calman was still fingering the stave, and he took the opportunity to change the subject. "Charlie, I would like to ask you something. Do you have a smell permeating your office from time to time?"

"Only when certain of my clients come in," he laughed. "Well there is an odour, like pastrami and sour pickles, that comes and goes. It seeps through the walls, and can be overpowering."

"Can't you do something about it?"

"What can I do?" asked Charlie, "It comes from the delicatessen next door. But wait until Thursday."

"What happens on Thursday?"

"Once a week, on each Thursday, the specialty of the house is corned beef and cabbage. Ahh! The cabbage aroma…it will take your breath away, fill every pore of your being. But the taste! I tell you, you'll never want to go home again to your mother's cooking."

Charlie saw that Calman was not amused.

"I'll tell you what," he said, "If you can't take the smell after a month, I'll let you out of the lease. Is that fair?"

Calman finished his bagel, and got up to leave.

"I think you like that stick," Charlie said thoughtfully. "Take it with you. It's yours."

"Thanks!" Calman was a collector of canes and walking sticks. He now had another one to add to his collection.

CHAPTER V

Calman sat at his desk, somewhat listless, unable to rouse himself out of his lethargy. Though he enjoyed the company and the humour of his new landlord, the whiff of corned beef and other deli aromas put him into ill humour. Two year-end files lay unopened on his desk.

He had recently acquired a habit of shutting out the world, and entering into a state of interior thought, where his mind rambled in free association from one idea to another. Now his mind was engrossed in the lost weekend he had spent with his friend Bennit, and his failed philandering in Muskoka. He had sure screwed it up for himself, and Bennit. Good thing that Bennit was a good sport, he thought. As he reflected about the embarrassing encounter with his client's daughter, he grew annoyed at himself, and then at the girl, too.

How could you hire this guy, Mencher, to be your auditor? Why don't you hire Bennit Moranz? He's so much smarter and he's on the ball, he imagined her berating her old man.

After a while, Calman's mood changed from one of bitterness to sadness, and then a kind of melancholia engulfed him. But, always the observer, in a self-conscious sort of way, he soon began to understand that his mood of despair was caused not by Miss Schwartz but by the alteration in nature which he had witnessed on his way back from the lodge. How quickly the scene had changed. And this led him to speculate on the transience of life, and then, by association, to the meaning of life, and then to his own life. Now he began to understand his mood – he was in a state of depression because his life had no meaning, no direction. But life has to be purposive. He had been reading Dostoevsky of late, and somehow had absorbed a few of his ideas.

Calman hated to admit to envy, but he now began to see that he was riddled with envy, especially of his friends who were already settled into family life. Jack Marcus was married, and had two kids. Saul Kimmel also had a family, and his wife Nancy was pregnant, again. Calman had been best man at Milton Pleat's wedding eight months ago and he, Calman, had not been able to get a date to bring with him. Now here he was, twenty-eight, and he couldn't even get laid. That was the missing dimension. There was no woman. He felt incomplete, and was yearning to be made whole.

Although Calman was seated at his desk, within easy grasp of the telephone, it rang three times before he was startled out of his reverie.

"Hello!" he intoned into the phone, affecting his best professional voice, posturing himself after Vince Saunders.

"May I speak to Mr. Mencher?"

The voice was thin, polite and feminine. His gloomy mood immediately evaporated, and was supplanted by a ubiquitous sense of pleasure. Calman was a man of instinct, and he often saw things whole rather than in fragments. It was thus that he immediately intuited a complete picture of the speaker. *She was a young woman, about twenty-five, intelligent, educated, an Oxonian, with the slightest inflection in her voice, suggesting a mid-European background, she had blue eyes, and she was unmarried—and probably uninitiated.*

"This is he," Calman replied.

"My name is Carole Williston," she said softly, seeming shy. "And you were referred to me by Mr. Maxwell Wolfe."

"Williston," Calman mused. He knew of a lawyer, Walter Williston.

No, he quickly swept away any connection between them. *Further, who is this Maxwell Wolfe?* He wondered.

She continued, "I am an oral surgeon, and I have started a practice at the Medical Arts Building. I am in need of an accountant to set up my records, and teach me how to maintain them. Would you accept me as a client?"

Would he accept her as a client? You betcha your life, lady.

"I would be delighted to, Doctor," he replied. "Where is your office?"

"I am in the Medical Arts Building at the corners of St. George and Bloor Streets. You can enter from St. George. My office is on the fifth floor."

"Well, that's very convenient. You're only a couple of blocks away from my office. Would tomorrow be all right?"

"Yes. I have some free time between one and two p.m. Will that be convenient?"

"Yes! Fine, I'll see you then."

Calman swiveled around in his chair and settled back. He was now brimming with a new energy and enthusiasm. He picked up the walking stick Charlie had given him, and addressed it, "Sir Stick, you have brought me luck. Thank you."

And he kissed the top of the cane.

One thing had puzzled Calman since the phone call from Dr. Williston. *Who was this Maxwell Wolfe?* He thought about it for a while, and finally it dawned on him. There was a Hermann Wolfe who had been a client of Vince Saunders. Hermann had a son, about Calman's age; whose name was Maxwell, and Calman now recalled having met him several times.

Maxwell was awkward, or so it seemed to Calman, but he could never quite figure out in what way. He did not give it much thought, but, come to think of it, Maxwell always did seem rather strange, sort of out of sync with the world. Calman also recalled that he would sometimes address Maxwell by the abbreviated moniker, Max, which always pleased Max, and which made him feel less estranged, as if he were one of the boys.

Calman now smiled inwardly, as he sat at his desk and thought of Max's father, Hermann Wolfe – an odd little man, not more than four feet ten inches, with a Pinocchio nose that came to a point at the tip, and a square head containing a tuft of reddish-orange disheveled hair, making him resemble a male raggedy Ann doll.

When Calman articled for Saunders, he had been assigned the Wolfe account. Hermann Wolfe, his wife and two sons, Max and Phillip, had immigrated to Canada from Czechoslovakia just before the outbreak of World War II. Mr. Wolfe was in the sand and gravel business, and he owned two gravel pits. Despite the fact that he was a shrewd businessman, Hermann had a number of idiosyncrasies, and whenever he made an appearance at the Saunders's offices, generally without an appointment, he drew smiles from the clerks and stenographers, in anticipation of some comical event about to take place.

Wolfe had obtained a permit allowing him to install gas tanks on the quarry sites for the exclusive use of trucks, tractors and bulldozers that operated on the site. These vehicles were not permitted off the site, nor were passenger vehicles permitted on the site. But sometimes, when no one was watching, Hermann would drive his own car into the pit and fill it up from the pump. The gas consisted of a low-grade octane, and he didn't realize that he was probably ruining the car engine. He was titillated by these mischievous antics, but was so busy watching out for anyone who might be watching him, that he became careless in handling the nozzle of the pump, with the inevitable result that, after each such episode, he was sodden with gasoline.

One day, Hermann came to see Calman, and as usual, he had not made an appointment. He was chewing on a cheap unlighted cigar, and was reeking of cheap gasoline. But Calman could not, at first, identify the stench. Some of the staff in the adjoining offices began holding their noses.

"How can I help you today Mr. Wolfe?" Calman asked him politely.

"I don't understand the statement you prepared for me. First, you tell me I am making money and den you tell me I am losing money. Please explain dis to me."

Calman did not want to take him into his own cubicle for fear Wolfe would smell up the office. Instead, he took him to the boardroom. He drew the file, and they sat down to review it.

"Now Mister Wolfe," he explained, "You produce five products – sand, two-inch stone, half-inch stone, pea gravel, and pit run. Is that right?"

Wolfe bit into his cigar in acknowledgment.

"Now, it is true that you are losing money on the pea gravel."

Wolfe jumped up, and with hands clasped behind his back, his torso bent forward, he started to pace, back and forth, the length of the room, crying, "I vill not sleep tonight! I vill not sleep tonight!"

"Yes," Calman interjected, "but you are making profits on the other four products. The net result of everything is a whopping profit. You should be very pleased."

The pacing became less frenzied, "Den I vill sleep tonight?" he asked meekly.

"You should sleep very soundly," Calman said in his most reassuring voice.

Wolfe followed Calman out into the reception room, and offered him a cigar. Calman pulled out his lighter, and was about to strike the flint, when Wolfe jumped into action. He dived over the desk, knocked over a chair and plant, and rolled on the floor. Suddenly it occurred to Calman that the foul odour was cheap gasoline. The commotion got everyone running from their offices. There was only one casualty - Elsie, the receptionist, laughed so hard, she was unable to hold her water as she went running to the ladies' room with a shriek.

Calman speculated that Hermann Wolfe must have come from another world, where he had been a leprechaun. Now, as he entered Dr. Williston's office, it also occurred to him that the foreign accent he had detected in her voice was Czech.

CHAPTER VI

Dr. Williston walked into the reception room to greet Calman. She was petite and charming, and except for the yellow ribbon holding her blonde hair in place she was entirely in white – crisp white smock tucked smartly into her girlish waist, pearl white buttons in a neat line running down the centre of her smock, white stockings, white shoes. She extended her hand at full arms-length.

"Hello!" her voice rang out in greeting. She was smiling cheerfully. Her handshake was firm. The grey-blue eyes, the radiant smile, the unrouged, but robust cheeks – she was a skier Calman decided– the delicate scent, the subtle outline of the two globes; he was unnerved. She was an innocent, all right. All of this was filtered through Calman's brain in a fraction of a second. *I wonder if she is sizing me up the same way*, he wondered. Calman pulled himself together, and banished his fantasies for the present.

Though he had already surmised the Wolfe connection, he politely enquired about both families. She was, he learned, an only child. She and her family had escaped from Czechoslovakia to England during the war. She had completed her medical degree in England. Her father, a physician, had died in England. Hermann Wolfe, an old friend from Prague, had persuaded her mother to immigrate to Canada after the war. Maxwell Wolfe, Hermann's older son, was her best friend, and they were planning a weekend excursion to Atlantic City.

That was it. Finito! He must drive away any thought of ever dating this alluring girl. That was now out of the question. Anything more than a handshake would be tantamount to a betrayal of the Wolfe family – like biting the hand that feeds you.

Calman now became more professional, and asked to see the doctor's records. They were quite skimpy – just a single entry. He had brought a binder with him, together with journal, and ledger sheets, which he inserted into the binder, and then gave her lesson number one in double-entry bookkeeping. He taught her how to make journal entries, and she was quick to catch on. She then showed him through her premises, which consisted of three operating rooms, and a waiting room. The latter included an area containing a counter and desk, at which the receptionist sat.

He made arrangements to return the following month, when he would review her entries and instruct her how to post to the ledger. She thanked him, and they shook hands. Calman walked back to his office, both exulted and dejected. *Carole Williston*, he mused, and tried to imagine Max making love to her, but could not conjure such a vision. There was something incongruous here. Max had always struck him as rather effete, sissified. Or were such thoughts just sour grapes on his part?

A month later, Calman telephoned his new client. The girlish voice was easily recognizable.

"Hello, Dr. Williston," he began.

"Oh, Mr. Mencher," she said sweetly, "Don't be so formal. Please call me Carole."

"OK," he quipped, "But only if you call me Calman, or Cal."

He was pleased that she had recognized his voice so readily. Their second meeting took place on the following day. Looking over her records, he noticed that she had followed his directions impeccably. While she tended to a patient in one of the operating rooms, Calman posted from the journals, which she had written up, to the ledger. When she returned, her assistant directed another patient into one of the other operating rooms while Dr. Williston sat down to talk to Calman. He gave her a quick lesson on how to make ledger entries. Again she demonstrated dexterity. She learned quickly.

He discovered that she had studied medicine at Cambridge in England, and dentistry in Toronto, and that she was the first woman oral surgeon in Canada. She also lectured to dental students at the University of Toronto. Calman was doubly impressed. They settled on an annual fee for his services, and agreed that he would meet with her twice each year, once midway through the year to discuss investments -- for it was apparent that she was going to be a high earner and would want to invest her savings -- and again at the end of the year to close out her books, prepare the financial statements, and file her income tax returns.

As Calman was about to leave, an elegant woman, past fifty, entered the room and smiled at him. Calman thought, *she must think I'm the doctor.*

"Oh, Calman," Dr. Williston stopped him. "I would like you to meet my mother."

"Well," he said, posturing old world chivalry. "It's indeed a pleasure to meet you, Mrs. Williston."

"The name is not Williston," she replied in a charming foreign accent, as she glanced askance at her daughter. "I am Mrs. Waitzer. I don't know a Mrs. Williston,"

He took the lady's extended hand, bent over it and brushed it with his lips. He wanted to say 'enchanté', but he knew instinctively that it would sound phony. As he held her hand, he had a strange but pleasing feeling that she was sizing him up approvingly. Out of the corner of his eye he saw Carole smile at him, and make a slight shrug.

There was no doubt in Calman's mind that a mutual attraction existed between himself and the doctor. Moreover, on a professional level, she respected him and had confidence in him.

Charlie Tepper was placing twelve per cent mortgages for his clients, and Calman asked him to place some for Dr. Williston. Charlie was only too pleased to oblige, and within a few months, she had built up a modest mortgage portfolio. Calman did not attempt to date her, nor did he make any advances, even discretely, but their relationship evolved into one of friendship, and occasionally teasing flirtations. They never talked about Max, but his haunting presence, it seemed to Calman, dampened these sessions. Their business sessions were sprinkled with personal contents. Sometimes, the talk turned to music or literature.

"Did you know," he asked her. "That the Israeli Symphony is going to be performing at the Massey Hall in Toronto?"

"Yes," she replied, "and I heard that Leonard Bernstein is coming over to conduct them. Are you going?"

He would have liked to be able to say: *I have a pair of tickets, would you like to join me?* But instead was compelled to say, "Unfortunately, I tried to get tickets a few days ago, but they were sold out."

The only touching between them was their handshake greetings; but these clasps came to be more and more like caresses.

One day, Calman was working in his office when he had an unexpected visitor, Hermann Wolfe.

"Mr. Wolfe," he exclaimed, standing up and exchanging a warm handshake. "It's been a long time, and it's so good to see you."

Mr. Wolfe was not a man to engage in frivolities. He got right to the point. "Mr. Mencher, I vant you should be my accountant."

Calman was pleased, but felt impelled to ask him, "Have you left Vince Saunders?"

"Not yet! I'm vaiting for your answer. If you do not take me, I vill go to somebody else."

"Are you not satisfied with Saunders's service?"

"I am not satisfied with Mr. Saunders. He is trying to steal my business."

Calman reflected. *This sounds like something that son-of-a-bitch would try to pull off.* "So why did you select me Mr. Wolfe?"

"Vhy not? I always liked you, and the way you used to handle my account, and besides, you come highly recommended by my goddaughter, Dr. Carole Vaitzer."

"Oh, you mean Dr. Williston."

"Vaitzer!" His voice had a ring of finality.

"You are right," he humoured the elderly gentleman.

Mr. Wolfe sniffed the air, "Pheeu! Vat is dat smell?"

Calman had become inured to the smells emanating from the delicatessen, and he no longer took any notice.

"Oh, that? It's from the restaurant next door. They make the best-corned beef and cabbage in the city. Come with me. You'll be my guest."

As they sat in the deli, enjoying a corned beef sandwich, and a beer, Calman asked Wolfe about his family. He was particularly interested in his son, Max.

"How is Max? What is he doing?"

He received a perfunctory "Nothing!" And Calman considered it best to pass on to another topic.

When Calman returned to his office, he decided to sit down, with a sense of pleasure, to draft a letter to his erstwhile employer, the slippery Vince Saunders:

Dear Sir:

Re Mr. Hermann Wolf, et al

Please take notice that we have been appointed auditors for the above-noted parties. If you know of any reason why we should not accept this appointment, please notify us at once.

Yours truly,

Having written the letter, Calman had a sense of uneasy anticipation about the irate phone call he would be receiving from Vince Saunders. He imagined their telephone confrontation.

Vince's voice would be all honey: "Hello Cal! How are you making out on your own?"

Calman would meet him on his own terms, honey for honey, "Why hello there! Is that you Vincent? It's so nice of you to call. Tell me, how are you making out since I left?"

"We're doing fine. You know, your junior partnership is still available for you. It always was."

"Now that's very generous of you. Is that why you called?"

"No! I called to help you out. I understand you would like to take over the Wolfe account. That's not a problem. In fact, I'm willing to give you several other accounts, which will form a solid base for your practice."

Calman was puzzled, not by Saunders's sudden burst of generosity, but because he could not figure out the catch.

"So what's the catch Vince?" He was taking pleasure in calling him by his given name. "Can you give me a list of the accounts you have in mind?"

Saunders read off the list. Calman recognized them – all accounts who never paid, or who were going out of business for one reason or another. Now came the real catch, "You will pay me a sum equal to one year's fees for each account."

"Quite frankly Vince," Calman said sarcastically. "My practice is growing so fast that I have no need to purchase someone else's practice. Is there something else you wanted to discuss with me?"

There was no answer at the other end, and Calman added peremptorily, recalling Saunders's words to him at their first interview,

"I guess that will be all." And he hung up.

Calman sat back, relaxed and pleased, and his mind returned to Mr. Wolfe. He knew that by accepting the Wolfe account, he had irrevocably ended any chance he might have for Carole Williston. He wondered whether shrewd Mr. Wolfe, sensing Carole's interest in him, had manipulated the situation so as to eliminate him from the running, for the sake of his son, Max.

CHAPTER VII

Serri Sturmac was an attractive and amiable woman of about forty, married to Harvey, a good-for-nothing, ill-mannered boor six years her senior; a man who fancied himself a ladies' man. Together, they owned a chain of retail ladies' ready-to-wear stores throughout the Province of Ontario, called Sturmac's.

The capital, which had funded the business, had come from the estate of Serri's parents. Harvey and Serri had each been issued one hundred common shares of the company, and Calman had been issued one common share in trust, to be used only in the event of a deadlock between the two principals. Serri possessed good taste, and she understood fashion. Harvey had enough good sense to let her do all the buying. He ran the operation and travelled to each store at least once a month. These excursions to the stores gave him the opportunity to indulge his pleasures – tippling, gambling and philandering. He hired each of the store managers, who were all good-looking, bosomy, and the adult-consenting type.

One day, Serri caught Harvey playing around with the bookkeeper, Gladys, and she promptly fired her. Once again, Harvey displayed great perspicacity – he did not interfere. Serri called up Calman, and asked him to teach her how to do the bookkeeping. He was very helpful, and soon they became friends. Serri felt maternal towards Calman, and on the days he came to review her work and balance the books, she would make sure to bring some of her home-cooked pastries for him.

It was the annual meeting for Sturmac's, and Calman had expropriated Harvey's large leather desk chair from which he conducted the meeting. Calman was well aware of Harvey's philandering, and he knew that it was damaging the business. He handed copies of the financial statements to each of the owners. "The company is losing money," Calman announced. "Sales are not only down from last year, but so are profit margins."

Serri interrupted, "I'm aware that sales have been going down, but why should the margins go down? I set all the prices myself and I know we should be earning a higher mark-up than you show. How do you account for it?"

Calman knew why profit margins were down. Harry was paying off his girlfriend managers from cash sales. They were probably stealing from the till, as well. Calman felt sorry for Serri.

"It could be that some pilfering is taking place, more than usual, or perhaps some cash is being skimmed off and the cash register tapes are being altered, or that you are giving too many discounts," Calman explained.

Serri was clearly upset. She turned to Harvey. "I told you so, but you wouldn't listen."

"Look!" said Calman, "Four of the stores are still profitable – Toronto, Hamilton, London and Windsor. They are located in the largest and most populous cities. All the others are in a downward spiral – Listowel, Ingersol, Oshawa, Lindsey, Peterborough, Guelph, Chatham, and so forth. You should consider closing up all the stores except the four in the larger cities."

"We have leases," Harvey complained, "Have you considered that we'll have to pay rent?"

"Why don't you have a talk with the landlords? Some may let you out of the lease with a small penalty. You may have a problem with the others.

Some of the stores you may be able to sub-lease. But, in any event, none of your leases has more than two years remaining."

Calman was only too well aware of Harvey's profligacy, and knew that his habit would not change. This was the first step to winding up the business with a minimum of damage, before everything was lost.

The meeting was adjourned, and Serri wrote out a cheque to Calman for his fees. Harvey grabbed the cheque out of her hands. "What is this?" he complained, "It's too much," and he tore it up. "What is the matter with you?" he asked his wife, "Make up a new one, and post-date it."

"No!" she said firmly. "He put in a lot of extra time teaching me how to do the bookkeeping. And he's worth a bonus." Staring angrily at her husband, whom she expected of wrongdoing, she added resentfully, "He does more for the business than you do." And she proceeded to rewrite the cheque. Harvey stalked out of the room.

There was an awkward silence, which Serri broke, "You are right, Calman. I can see the direction this business is taking, and don't think that I'm not aware of what is going on."

Calman felt sorry for her. She walked to her desk and opened the top drawer, and pulled out an envelope.

"Calman, I have two tickets to *The Glass Menagerie*, you know, the play by Tennessee Williams. It's being performed at the Royal Alex Theatre. We have a family anniversary party that night and cannot go. I thought you might be able to use them. It's a shame they should go to waste."

"Yes, I know the play, but I've never seen it." Calman said, accepting the tickets.

CHAPTER VIII

One day each week Calman allowed himself the luxury of having lunch at Harry's Delicatessen. He was seated by himself reading the *Globe and Mail*, which someone had conveniently left on the chair. Harry came over wearing an apron and a chef's hat.

"What'll it be today?" Calman looked over the menu, which he already knew.

"Let me see," he mused as he fingered the menu, "How about a corned beef on rye, French fries, a couple of dills and a coke."

"Okay, the usual," said Harry.

Calman bit into his sandwich while reading the paper, and heard a familiar voice, "Would you like some company?" It was Sally, his landlord's receptionist. Before he could answer her, she was already sitting down and beckoning Harry.

"So, Calman," She said, "How's it going?"

"OK." he answered noncommittally.

"OK is not an answer. Besides I'm not talking about business. In business, you'll be all right. Charlie has already recommended you to two of his clients, and you're going to be hearing from my husband, Al Nodal. Al is starting up in a small way to manufacture children's wear."

Calman regarded this woman who sat opposite him, munching on her sandwich. He estimated her age as just under fifty, she was a frumpy blonde, or maybe a brunette, with wide hips, and a good-natured soul. "I was talking about your personal life," she said.

"What about my personal life?"

"Are you thirty yet?"

"I'm twenty-eight.

"And do you still live at home with mama and papa?"

"As a matter of fact I do." He was embarrassed, so he added: "I save a lot of money that way."

"Move out," was her terse rejoinder. "Venture on your own. It's time. Do you have a sweetheart?"

"Now you're really prying."

"Do you mean that I'm getting too personal?"

"Yes, that's right."

"So what of it? It's personal-shmersonal! Do you have a girlfriend?"

"Well, there is a lady I'm interested in."

Calman told her about his attraction to Dr. Williston, and the reason for his hesitation about asking her for a date.

"But you really like this girl, and you have strong vibes that she likes you?"

He nodded.

"Then don't be a fool. Ask her out. You have no proof that she's engaged to this guy, Max, or even in love with him."

"But it's not fair. It is *because* of Max that she is my client."

Sally finished her lunch, and got up to leave. She patted Calman on the head.

"So, what! You know what they say – All's fair in love and war!" and she was out the door. Calman sat there for a few more minutes, reflecting. Now it came to him – the ancient axiom – *Carpe diem* – Seize the day."

CHAPTER IX

Six months had elapsed since Calman's last meeting with Dr. Williston, and he was looking forward to another business rendezvous with her. He dialled Carole's number, and was greeted by her receptionist, a middle-aged matron.

"Is Dr. Williston in?" he enquired.

"Oh! Hello Mr. Mencher." He was pleased that she had recognized his voice. "Dr. Williston is with a patient right now. Can she call you back, say, in half an hour?"

Hmmm! he mused, *That's unusual. She usually interrupts her work to take my call.*

Instead of turning his attention to other matters, he sat at his desk thinking about how he would go about inviting her to join him at the Royal Alex to see the Tennessee Williams play. He was not absolutely certain about her feelings for Max, and he could test the waters by merely offering her the tickets.

Perhaps you and Max would care to see the play. I'm tied up that evening. No! That would not do...too contrived.

Besides, he was now beginning to believe that she and Max were indeed only friends, and nothing more. After all, she never spoke of him. Then again, he could be casual about the invitation. *I happen to have a pair of tickets to The Glass Menagerie. If you're free would you care to join me?* Should he ask her during their telephone conversation, or wait until he saw her at her office?

A full hour elapsed before Carole returned his call.

"Hello, Cal." The buoyant voice lifted his spirits. They chatted for a few minutes, and Calman grew more confident, taking the lead in the conversation. He felt more than ever that they were *en rapport*. He thought, *Carpe diem! I'll ask her out right now.*

"Carole…" but before he could get the words out, a great chasm opened, and he was in a free fall.

"You know Cal," she said, "I'm married now."

A sensation of dank cold descended over his body. *Had he died?* He wondered. A stunned silence set in, the kind of quiet before a storm, a tornado.

Finally, she said: "Cal, are you there?"

"Well! Ahh! Ahh! Congratulations," he managed to splutter. He was in turmoil. Bees were swarming in his head. "You must convey my best wishes to Max."

"Max!" she exclaimed with surprise, and laughing. "No, I'm not married to Max. Didn't you know that Max is a homosexual? My husband's name is Kenneth Hughes, but I intend to retain my maiden name for professional reasons. Ken is a pilot with Trans Canada Airlines. That's how we met. I was on a trip to London to visit some old friends, and Ken was the pilot."

She rambled on…something about being pregnant, and having purchased a home in the Hamilton Mountain area, but Calman was in a daze, and her words did not register above his sub-conscious level. She repeated her earlier words: "Cal, are you there?"

Calman roused himself from his somnolent trance.

"Yes, yes," he said hurriedly. "I'm here. I'm just trying to let it all sink in. So, uhh, you're married. You've purchased a new home. Did you say you're with child? It must have all been very sudden."

"Yes," she replied, "I left for England on the day following our last meeting, about six months ago. During a coffee break, when the co-pilot took over the controls, Ken came ambling down the passenger cabin, and he saw me sitting there reading a magazine. He was all smiles, and he introduced himself. He was so debonair in his captain's uniform. I think it was love at first sight. We were married two months later. It was a whirl-wind courtship."

There was a little more chatter. She provided Calman with some details about her new home. She also informed him that her lease at the Medical Arts Building was expiring, and that she intended to move her practice to her home. She invited him to come to her new home to perform the annual audit. Carole seemed very excited about having Calman meet her husband. "I've told Kenny all about you, and he's looking forward to meeting you."

After they had finished the conversation, and the phone had been returned to its cradle, and the turmoil that had swept through Calman's brain had settled down, he leaned back in his swivel, a habit he had picked up when he had need to cogitate. He filled his pipe with an aromatic tobacco, lit up, tamped it down, and took in a long puff.

How could he have missed all the signs? He had been misled by the Max factor – ha, ha – the unintended pun was there. When Wolfe had offered him his account, he had had the temerity to imagine that it was a bribe to stay away from Carole. Wolfe was her godfather, and Calman now realized that what Wolfe wanted was for her to meet a nice young man with prospects, who would make a good husband for her. Calman was probably his choice, but Calman had failed to pick up the numerous hints given by Mrs. Waitzer, Mr. Wolfe, even Carole herself. Even his own instincts had betrayed him.

CHAPTER X

Bennit picked up the phone, and listened for a few moments.

"Just a minute! I have to clean the wax out of my ears. Ahh! That's better. Now I can hear. You know, for a moment you sounded just like a guy I used to know. His name is Cal Mencher."

Calman chuckled. "How is my old tennis partner? I hear that your tennis game is getting to be as bad as your gin rummy."

"And who would you have heard that from?" asked Bennit. They both chuckled.

"I've tried to call you several times," said Bennit, "but I've had no success. Either your line is busy, or you're out of the office."

"Why don't you leave a message?"

"Well, it was not important. I just wanted to know how you are making out in your new office setup."

"The practice is growing. In fact, I'm thinking of articling a student. Say, if you're free tomorrow evening, why not join me for dinner?"

"Gee! I've got a date tomorrow night, and I'm also booked for Thursday. But I'm free on Friday. What do you say for Friday?"

"I'm sorry, "said Calman dejectedly: "I can't make it on Friday. Perhaps we can get together one evening next week."

"Say Cal, you sound somewhat downcast. What happened? Did the cat die? Did you lose your biggest client?"

"No, it's not anything like that! I'm OK."

"You sure?"

"Of course I'm sure. I'll see you next week." They hung up.

Calman reached into the breast pocket of his jacket where he kept a little black book containing a list of his friends, men and women, in alphabetical order. As he withdrew the book, a little white envelope fell out. He opened the envelope to find the two theatre tickets, which Serri Sturmac had given him.

He flipped the pages of the book and came to the letter 'D', and he began to scan the page. *Dunne...Marie Dunne.* Why hadn't he thought of her sooner? He dialled her number. After a couple of rings, the familiar cheerful voice answered. "Hello-o!" the voice sang. Calman's mood began to change. He already felt uplifted.

"Hello, Marie!"

"Calman Mencher! Is that you?"

"Why?" he laughed, "Were you expecting someone else?"

"No!" she replied. "I've been sitting here waiting for your call for weeks. It's so good to hear from you. How is the new practice?"

"It's growing, Marie. It's growing. And how is the dancing instructor?"

"I can teach you to waltz, to shimmy, to fox-trot, to one-step, to two-step, to cha cha...would you like a lesson?"

Calman was beginning to enjoy himself.

"You know," he said. "I would love to learn those steps, but I really called you for another reason. I have theatre tickets for Thursday evening for *The*

Glass Menagerie. It's playing at the Royal Alex. How about having dinner with me first, and then going to the theatre?"

"I usually work evenings," she demurred. A look of disappointment crossed his brow. "But Thursday is my night off. I would be delighted." He was relieved she had not seen his vulnerability.

Calman arrived at Marie's home at six o'clock. This would give them enough time for dinner, and conversation, before curtain time. Her residence was quite small, he thought, tucked in between two grand old houses of nineteenth century vintage. There was no visible number on the house, and he thought he might be in the wrong place. But suddenly a light went on, and Marie emerged.

"Good evening, Cal. You are in the right place. Did you have difficulty finding it?" She looked stunning, dressed in a black skirt and jacket, a twilled blouse, and a velvet tam tilted at a saucy angle on her voluptuous black mane.

"No, Marie. But it's a rather quaint house you live in."

"Well, it's not your regular kind of house. In fact, it's called a coach house and it's owned by my neighbour. At one time, during the last century, it was a stable, and it actually housed horses."

"Could be an artist's digs," he commented. Marie took his arm and he led her to the car. As she was climbing into the bucket seat he remarked, "Marie, you're looking beautiful. I guess that dancing agrees with you."

She gave him a beaming smile.

They were seated in a cozy corner of the restaurant. Calman selected a French red wine, and they both ordered Rock Cornish Hen. The conversation flowed easily. First they talked about dancing.

"Have you given any thought to ballet?" he asked her.

"Ballet is a completely different kind of dance. It is classical and takes years of training. I'm far too old for that. Besides, I think that the popular kind of dance is much more accessible to the average person, and a lot more fun. You would be surprised at the variety of people, from different walks of life, men and women of all ages, who come to the studio for lessons and enjoyment. Now tell me Cal Mencher, what have you been up to?"

"Well, let's see now. I've been working hard. The practice has been growing. I've been taking courses in English Lit."

"That was your first love, wasn't it?"

"I guess you can say that."

"And the other kind of love? What about that?"

"And what kind would that be?"

Calman was a little disconcerted by her observation. He thought to himself: *She's very perceptive*. He quickly changed the subject. "Say, do you remember Hermann Wolfe?"

"Of course I do!" she replied. "He was the funny little man with the gravel pits."

"He left Vince Saunders and became my client."

"Good for him, and good for you. You were the only one in the office who knew how to handle him." Then, after a pause in the conversation, Maria asked him, "Do you know why I left Vince?"

"I thought it was because you wanted a change – to become a dancing teacher."

Marie shook her head.

"One evening I worked late. Vincent had a lot of dictation to get out. There were only the two of us in the office. He had been working in his office, and I was in mine, typing away. After a while he came from his inner sanctum, as you used to call it, and asked me how long it would take to finish my work. Then he came up behind me and stood for a while watching me type. He made me feel very uncomfortable, breathing down my neck. The next thing I knew he was caressing my back. I jumped up and faced him. 'Don't do that Mr. Saunders,' I said. 'Aw, come on,' he said, and he put his hand on my breast. I backed away, grabbed my hat and my purse, and rushed out. I wasn't afraid of him. He's the one who was scared.

"The next morning I came to the office as usual. Alex and Clifford were there. I walked right into his office without so much as a by your leave. 'Mr. Saunders,' I told him – I guess I was a little emotional because my cheeks felt as though they were on fire, though I felt quite calm – 'I cannot work for you anymore. I'm giving you two weeks' notice, which is more than fair, considering the circumstances.' He became flushed, but did not utter a word."

"I always knew that Vince was a cad," said Calman. "He was slick. Little did I suspect that he was also slime. I'm surprised that he didn't try to talk you into staying on."

"No!" Marie said darkly. "He knew he had crossed the line."

After dinner, they walked across the street to the theatre, and were ushered to their seats, centre orchestra. Marie was pleased, and Calman thought to himself, "Boy, Serri Sturmac has expensive taste."

Driving back to Marie's home Calman asked her how she had enjoyed the play.

"Heavy stuff!" she said.

"Yes," he agreed. "Tennessee Williams reminds me a little of Chekov."

"I don't know much about Chekov. In what way do you think they're alike?"

"Chekov writes about characters that are – well – lonely and also isolated. So does Williams. I think that Williams' two best plays are the one we saw this evening and *A Streetcar Named Desire*. In both of them, the main characters are on the fringe of society, both pine for a time past, and which is lost to them."

"Where did they get the title *Glass Menagerie*?"

"Well, Laura, the protagonist in the plot, was crippled and could not live up to her mother's expectations. No one gave her any sympathy or understanding, so she took comfort in her collection of glass animals. This glass menagerie is fragile, and thus serves as a symbolic reminder of the girl's own predicament – her vulnerability."

"Cal," Marie answered, "I'm not too knowledgeable about literature. As a young girl I read *Wuthering Heights* and I also read *Jane Eyre*. And that's about it."

"A hell of a great start!" he said.

"I don't care for those novels in which real people or ideas are represented by symbols."

"OK. So what do you like?"

"Just straight drama – boy meets girl, family tries to break them up, they elope. They live happily. The End!"

Now she was giggling.

Calman smiled as he recalled the verse from his sophomore days in tortured English-Latin:

Boyabus kiss-bus girlabus in parlor-um,

Girlabus like-a-bus, Wantum somorum.

Intraire pater into parlor-um,

Kick-a-bus boyabus out-a-bus doorum.

They arrived at Marie's home, and Calman parked his car out front. On his way down to call for Marie, he had come from the north, where the terrain was more or less flat, and he had not noticed that her home was located at the top of a steep embankment. The road commenced running downhill from a point adjacent to her home. Returning to her home after the theatre, they came from the south, and he had to put his car into second gear in order to climb the hill. He now went around to the passenger side and opened the door.

Marie slid out and said, "Would you like to come in, and I'll fix you a drink?"

Calman looked at his watch. It was after one o'clock, and he had an early morning meeting.

"Thank you Marie," he said, "But it's rather late. I think I should go home. It's been a wonderful evening."

He bent forward to kiss her on the cheek. She too bent forward, but faced him frontally, and in a moment they were in an embrace, clinging to one another, mouth to mouth. Before he could pull back, her tongue entered his mouth, and began exploring its inner regions. He instinctively responded. He was hard. Suddenly she let out a scream. He looked up.

"Oh! Damn!"

His car was rolling backward down the hill. It was going to crash. He rushed after the car, which came to a halt at the bottom of the street against a tree. He inspected the car, and breathed a sigh of relief. There was only a minor scratch. He got into the car and drove back up. This time, when he parked, he ensured that the brake was on and that the wheel was turned so that if the car moved, it would go into the curb. Marie giggled.

"Cal, you should have seen yourself racing the car. Did you ever think of trying out for the Olympics? I think you could use the drink I promised."

"OK."

They went in, and talked for a while, but Calman had spent his passion on the damn car, and he could not re-ignite it now.

CHAPTER XI

Calman completed his review of Dr. Williston's file, placed the documents he would require for their meeting in his briefcase, and set out to visit his client at her new offices, in the Hamilton Mountain. Although he had written down the directions, he became confused by the assortments of roads, streets and crescents, all bearing the same name.

At last he found her home – a large, rambling brown-brick bungalow on a very amply treed lot. He recognized several species of trees – evergreens, a blue spruce, an elm, four white pines, several maples, even a chestnut tree. He was still cataloguing them when the door opened. Carole looked radiant as she extended her hands to greet him. She had never, it seemed to him, been so effusive, nor had she ever exhibited such warmth towards him as she was at that moment.

Is she patronizing me? He asked himself. But then, again, she was also acting playful – another side of her he had never seen. Walking ahead of him, side-wise, like a little girl, her hand clasped in his, she led him into the living room.

"Ken," she called proudly, as if showing off a prize horse, "Come here, and meet Calman."

The man strode in.

"Calman, this is my husband, Kenneth. Ken, this is my favourite financial adviser, auditor and friend, Cal Mencher."

Calman looked up…up…up. The man was at least six foot six. Calman's hand disappeared into the giant's palm. Ken was athletic-looking, and he was tanned, and handsome. Two furry brows shadowed his embedded eyes. A thicket of black hair crowned his head; a dimple, which accentuated his good looks, marked the middle of Ken's chin. Calman took an instant dislike to the man.

Carole excused herself and went into the kitchen to brew a pot of tea, intending to give the two men an opportunity to get better acquainted, but actually leaving an awkward silence. The moments ticked away, but each waited for the other to speak. Calman imagined two boxers circling one another, waiting for an opening, except that it would only take a flick of Ken's finger to send Calman into orbit. He immediately sized Ken up as a redneck, and wondered how Carole could have become so infatuated with him. Calman tried to infuse a little enthusiasm into the dense and cloddish atmosphere.

"I understand you're a pilot," he offered.

"Yeah!" came the monosyllabic response.

Calman tried again. "It sounds exciting."

"Yeah. I guess."

"Where do you generally fly?"

"Jamaica."

"I thought you flew to London."

"Sometimes."

"What's it like in Jamaica?"

"Hot."

Calman asked the uni-word man how long he had been flying.

"Thirteen years!"

He had done it. Calman claimed the credit. The man had uttered two words in succession.

"Do you enjoy flying?"

"Yeah."

Oh! Oh! He's regressing – back to one word. There was another lull, and Calman felt as if a curtain of mist was descending. He had to do something fast. So he told him a joke.

"There was an Englishman, a Frenchman and a Jew…" Kenneth slapped his thighs and laughed tumultuously.

After the hysterics caused by the joke, Kenneth settled down and enquired curiously: "Are you Jewish?"

"Yes, I am!"

"Gee, I never met a Hebrew before."

The little hairs on the back of Calman's neck began to tingle, and his defences went into action.

"And you?" Calman asked, "What are you?"

The irony went over Ken's head.

"Carole and me are both Anglicans."

Calman said nothing. Carole came back into the room, obviously pleased that the two were getting on so well. She rolled in a small trolley containing a pot of tea, elegant chinaware, and two silver trays on which were laid out little sandwiches and French pastries. Calman eyed his favourite pastry, a Napoleon. But he hesitated, not quite sure of the protocol. Would it be in poor taste to reach for the Napoleon? But even as he wondered, Ken's large hand reached over and grabbed it. He devoured it with two bites, and followed it up by licking his fingers.

Son-of-a-bitch! Calman screamed the expletive inwardly. *First, he steals my girl and then he steals my favorite pastry…*

He was unsure of whether he had been heard, but the displeasure on his face did not escape Carole, and she urged him to try one of the other pastries.

No! He was going to embarrass Ken for his boorishness by a display of impeccable manners. Controlling his desire for a pastry, he accepted one of the dainty sandwiches instead, and ate it with mincing bites, while he sipped his tea with poised pinkie. As a further putdown, he turned, facing Carole, and blocked Ken's view of her. But neither his exaggerated manners nor his occlusion tactic had any effect on Ken.

"Got any more of them éclairs?" he asked, standing up and looking over the tray.

"Napoleons," Carole corrected him, smiling. "No dear, but if you like them, I'll buy some next time I visit the patisserie."

Calman completed his review of Dr. Williston's accounts, and then gathered up some of her records, which he packed into his briefcase. He felt uncomfortable with Ken hovering around, looking over his shoulder, and was anxious to leave. Also, he would now be able to complete the work at leisure in his office. He noted that the house had been purchased with Carole's funds, and that the lawyer handling the transaction had had the good sense to register the title in her name.

Before leaving, Carole insisted on giving him a tour of the house and grounds. Ken sauntered behind, hands in pockets. After showing Calman through the house, she led him into the garden.

"It's a beautiful house," he remarked. "And the garden is lovely. I hope you enjoy it here, and I wish you much happiness."

He noticed a particular flower that was blossoming in different sections of the garden – compact ball-shaped plants covered with rich indigo blue flowers, about six inches in height.

"What are these?" he asked.

"Oh! They're my favourite. I've had them sprinkled throughout the garden. They're of a genus technically called Myosotis-Alpestris, Blue Ball flowers, commonly called forget-me-nots."

Forget-me-nots? How ironic, he thought.

Ken had not followed them outside, and when they reversed their steps to go back into the house, he was not in sight, though Calman thought that he was within earshot.

"Well, Cal," she asked him, anxious for approval. "How do you like my husband?"

He could not think of anything complementary to say.

"I think he's a very lucky man," he said. There! He had deftly parried the question, but it was an embarrassing moment. She quickly switched to a neutral subject.

"Have you been to the symphony?"

"Yes, I have season's tickets. So I rarely miss a concert,"

Ken entered the room as Calman was preparing to take his leave.

"Ken, dear," Carole moved over to her husband and took his hand, "Calman is leaving us now."

They accompanied Calman to the door. As they entered the vestibule, Calman noticed a solitary cane cocked up in an umbrella stand. It was composed of a single stock of bamboo. The grip was curled and thick, and the shaft tapered down gradually. He picked it up. It was buoyant. He ran his fingers up and down its length, and he was reminded of the cane that had served as a prop for Charlie Chaplin. Turning his feet outward, duck-style, he shuffled forward a few steps, and gave the cane a couple of twirls. Ken, standing with hands in his pockets, laughed heartily. Carole giggled with delight. The tension was broken. Calman returned the cane to its stand, and departed.

CHAPTER XII

The tennis club was being sold to a developer, and this meant that Calman and Bennit would have to find another locale to engage in their favorite sport. Some of the members were already talking about buying a parcel of land, and building their own courts, and a clubhouse. Both Bennit and Calman had been invited to attend a meeting to discuss the idea of relocating the club, but the meeting ended, with nothing resolved, and it was never reconvened. In the meantime, the old club celebrated the end of that era with a bang-up party. No shorts were allowed. The women had to wear skirts or dresses, the men, jackets. It was at this party that Calman met Ruth.

The moment Calman set eyes on Ruth, he lost his senses. All evening, he seemed to be in a haze. He monopolized her, and danced every dance with her, or rather floated through each dance. Fortunately she had come to the dance with another girl friend, who was a member of the club, and with whom Bennit was now preoccupied.

It was only after he had escorted Ruth home, and she allowed him to kiss her that he attempted, with his accountant's mind, to add up her attributes. First, he was struck by her posture. Whether she sat, stood or walked she bore herself erect, head high, not bolt upright – she was too feminine for that – rather like a ballet dancer.

One day, after Calman had become a regular at Ruth's home, her mother, Pearl, confided to him that as young girl, Ruth would practise for hours walking in the hallways, and up and down the stairs with a book balanced on her head. He also noted that she was extremely light on her feet, especially when they danced. She seemed to trip the light fantastic as though her feet never touched the dance floor, and it was only when he complimented her on being the lightest, smoothest partner he had ever danced with, that she confided to him that she had studied the Martha Graham technique of modern dance.

"How about a demonstration?" he asked her.

"Later," she promised.

Calman then started to appraise her physical qualities. Her cheekbones were high, and they reminded him of etchings he had seen of ancient Egyptian princesses. Her eyes were cerulean blue, the colour of the sky on a clear sunny day. But he had seen blue eyes before. These radiated with intelligence. She possessed, it seemed to him, ample breasts, which he had brushed against as they danced, and she had an hourglass figure with a slender waist. But it was her wit, and humour, that most captured Calman's admiration. She could turn a phrase with refined delicacy.

One evening, after having dined with one of her loquacious friends, Cynthia Harris, Calman remarked, "That woman did not stop talking all evening. She refused to come up for air."

"Yes," Ruth answered, "A veritable Niagara."

She was also an insatiable reader. She devoted every spare minute to reading, and could draw on a vast source of knowledge in areas of literature, art, history and philosophy as well as palaeontology. She could rhyme off a long list of prehistoric mammals, which never ceased to amaze Calman.

During one of their long walks, when Calman was courting her, he put the question to her, "Apart from religion do you have a philosophy?"

"I guess so," she said.

Calman waited expectantly. Finally, changing the subject, she observed, "The sky is very starry tonight. Do you know which one is the Big Dipper?"

"I think so," he said, wondering if she was testing him. He then repositioned himself behind her, and pointing his right index finger over her right shoulder toward the sky, and squeezing her left shoulder.

"Do you see that very bright star over to the right?" She nodded. "It is called Polaris or The North Star. Now imagine a line inclining gradually down. Follow my finger. That is the tail of the Little Dipper. Do you see?" She nodded.

"Now do you see a cluster of stars from the end of the tail?" She nodded again. He then drew a rectangle in the air.

"That rectangular constellation is Ursa Minor, commonly called 'the Little Dipper.'"

Calman was enjoying the contact with Ruth. He allowed his left hand to squeeze her shoulder and to caress it. It was so soft. She too enjoyed the sensation.

"Now, let your eye follow a line beneath the Little Dipper." Again pointing upwards, his finger sketching out another rectangle in the air, "That constellation is called Ursa Major, or as you call it the 'Big Dipper.'"

"I see," she said thoughtfully, and then as an afterthought, "How did you acquire all this knowledge about the stars?"

"Oh!" Calman was nonchalant, "I took a course in astronomy during my first year at Varsity, but I hated doing logarithms, and dropped it in the second year."

They walked on for a while, arm in arm, without a word being spoken. Suddenly Ruth broke the silence. "Emulate Socrates."

"What did you say? … Emulate Socrates?"

"Yes! That's my philosophy...and what is yours?"

"Does that mean that you are argumentative?" he teased.

"No," she was quick to respond. "But I do believe that finding right answers demands asking right questions."

Pausing for a moment, she continued, "and you, what about your philosophy?"

"I'm still working on that. At best, I've got a few rules, such as work hard, play hard. Develop a close relationship with a few friends, enjoy a hobby."

"That is very commendable for a man who's still working on it. And do you have a hobby?"

"Yes. I collect canes."

"Do you mean walking sticks?"

"I do."

"Hmm! I must inspect my father's cane," she mused.

Calman started to court Ruth seriously. He felt more than ever that they were *en rapport*. One evening, the pair returned from an evening at the symphony, and Ruth invited Calman in. Her father, Reb Fischel, had emigrated from Poland in 1931, and had worked in his brother-in-law's sweatshop until he had saved enough to send for his wife, and their two children. Both of Ruth's parents spoke English with a heavy Yiddish accent, and they never minced words.

Ruth introduced Calman: "This is my friend, Calman Mencher."

The mother sized him up quickly, "Vot happened to Mr. Fucks."

"Fox!" Ruth quickly interjected.

"Dat's vot I said…Fucks."

Calman smiled. Her father was the more practical one.

"Vot do you do for a living?"

"I'm an accountant," he replied expectantly.

Reb Fischel grunted.

"Vhy can't de modern boys do something vorth vhile, like a furrier or a butcher?"

The question was rhetorical and was ignored by the young couple. The father continued, "From dis vork you do, can you make a living?"

"Yes!" Calman replied, a little facetiously. "Almost as much as a furrier."

Reb Fischel then announced unceremoniously, "It's very late. It's time for bed," and his hint to leave was not lost on Calman. His wife sauntered after him, but before exiting the room she turned around and said, "It vas nice to meet you, Mr. Menchen."

"Mencher!" Ruth corrected her.

Although Ruth was a free spirit, and did pretty much as she pleased, she nevertheless observed the one house rule, and did not invite Calman into her room. Instead, despite her father's injunction, she led Calman into the living room, where she let down her hair, and performed the promised free-style, sensual dance for him, which she concluded by throwing herself into his arms, which were waiting to embrace her. And they made love there, on the rug, in the living room. Calman had not expected things to progress so quickly, and he lay beside Ruth luxuriating in the joy of her physical presence.

This is instinct, he thought, *experienced only in Eden*. All other thought was abandoned. Suddenly, at midnight, an alarm clock went off.

"What's that?"

"That's a message from my father telling you that it's time to leave."

The next day Ruth's father admonished her, "Vhy vas dis boy here so late?"

She answered him defiantly, "He's not a boy. He's a man. And we were necking."

And he grumbled back.

"Vhat? Mit a new boy you vas necketing?"

CHAPTER XIII

Calman was now spending each evening with Ruth. When he thought the moment was right he sent her a single yellow rose, which, he had learned, was her favourite flower. On the following day he sent her two yellow roses, and on the third day three. He kept this up until the twelfth day when he personally presented her with a dozen yellow roses. Then he asked her to be his wife.

"I'm not sure if I am ready to get married," Ruth told him.

"But I thought you loved me," he spoke hesitatingly because he was in shock.

"I do love you," she replied. "But I'm not sure that I want to marry yet."

"Surely, Ruth, my proposal does not come as a big surprise."

"No, it does not, but now that I am confronting the prospect…" her voice trailed.

"Ahh!" he tried to assure her, "You're having some ambivalence. Of course, that is only natural. All right," he was resigned, "we'll talk about it again soon."

On the following day Ruth called Calman. "Can you come over Cal? We need to talk."

He selected a walking stick from his cane collection and was at her door in fifteen minutes. They went out for a walk. Calman strode along swinging his cane. Ruth seized his arm, and held on in order to keep pace with him. He remained silent, waiting for her to initiate the subject. After a while she pleaded out of breath. "Please slow down. I can't keep up with you."

He slacked off to a slow walk. "Is that better?"

"Yes, much better," she paused to gather her thoughts, and after a few moments, she said, "Cal, as you know, I spent the last two years in Philadelphia."

"Yes, I know. You were taking a Master's Degree at the University of Pennsylvania."

"During my stay there I made some friends with whom I became quite attached. There was Olga Stehlik, with whom I shared a room, and Gary Korman, her boyfriend. The three of us were taking the same courses and we often studied together. Have you ever heard of Anais Nin?"

"I don't believe so."

"Well, she is the most famous patient of Otto Rank. She was also his disciple. I suspect she may have been his mistress as well. And she was also an accomplished writer."

"And who is this Otto Rank?"

"He is a world renowned psychoanalyst, and a very close friend of Freud."

"Are you referring to Sigmund?"

"Yes, Sigmund Freud. Well, anyway, Anais came to our school to give a lecture. After her talk the three of us – Olga, Gary and I – cornered her, and we went out to lunch. I think she took a fancy to us because she invited us to join her at her hotel suite the next day. She was charming, beautiful and vivacious, and also very, very neurotic. But we loved her, and the three of us became members of the Otto Rank Society."

Calman interjected.

"You were in the company of some pretty high-powered people. I am not in their league. But somehow, I thought we were going to talk about us. What does all this have to do with us? Or is there something that I am missing?"

"Cal, I'm coming to that. You see Gary's best friend was a chap by the name of Paul Frankfurter."

"Any relation to Felix Frankfurter, the U.S. supreme Court Justice?" Calman was curious to know.

"I believe he is an uncle."

"All right! So what about this Paul?"

"We became very good friends."

"I see!" He said in a sarcastic tone. "Do you mean lovers?"

"Yes!" Her voice trembled as she uttered that single word. It was more a sob than an utterance, and it embodied all her worries and fears, as she foresaw the end of her hopes. They walked on in silence for a while. It was late September, and autumn was in the air.

"Do you still love him?" The question was put with resignation.

"I don't know. I don't think so. But…" There was no need to complete the question. "But I have to return to Philadelphia in order to find out so that I can bring closure to the relationship."

They continued to walk for a while, and Calman was conscious that they were no longer holding hands. He felt a chill as a depression descended on him. But he said nothing. At last Ruth broke the silence.

"And so I am leaving tomorrow by train." Calman knew that it would be unwise to try to talk her out of going. "All right," he offered. "I'll drive you to Union Station."

CHAPTER XIV

Calman selected the mahogany cane, with the silver handle crooked into the shape of an elephant's face, complete with tusks and trunk, and started on his walk. He ambled along without following any specific path. His destination was mental, not physical. He needed to do some cogitating, some soul searching.

Why is it that nothing comes easily to me? Why is it that when something good comes along, I cannot hold onto it?

Calman recalled his days in Verdun, a small town bordering the city of Montreal, when he was nine years old. He was the only Jewish boy in the school, and a well-meaning teacher, wanting to motivate her unmanageable pupils to try harder, promised a dime to the boy who came first in the class. At the end of the month, as the children were being dismissed for the Christmas holidays, she handed out the report cards, admonishing the class:

"Shame on all of you for allowing the Jewish boy to beat you. Stand up, Calman Mencher, and come to the head of the class."

A frightened Calman stood up, and shuffled to the front of the room, to receive the dime. No sooner were the children dismissed than the class rowdies grabbed Calman, trounced him, and took the dime.

He recalled a time, during his seventeenth year, when he was in his last year of high school. He belonged to a prestigious boys' club, and for the first time in the four-year history of the club, the members were going to have a mixed party. Each club member was expected to bring a date to the party. Calman had met Stella Rabin at his school, a pretty blond, and he asked her to be his date for the occasion. He was pleased that she had accepted, but as the day of the party grew nearer, he began to have misgivings about her. He heard rumours that she smoked, and was considered loose.

His friend, Jack Mintz, chided him.

"This dame is dumb. Do you understand what I'm saying? Dumb! Dumb! Dumb! She probably won't last to graduation. You are a scholarship boy, the school-debating champion. You write poetry. What will you talk to her about…how to parse a sentence?"

"It's too late," Calman, replied calmly. "I've already asked her to be my date, and I can't break my promise."

The evening before the party, Calman phoned Stella and told her that he would pick her up at seven p.m. The following evening, Calman arrived at his date's home five minutes before seven. He waited downstairs for the five minutes to elapse. During the wait, he noted that twenty-six snow-laden stairs led up to the door entrance.

There must be ice under some of those stairs. Someday, someone will slip and have a serious accident.

The five minutes were up. He bounded up the stairs, two at a time. He hesitated for a moment, and then rang the bell. A frumpy-looking, middle-aged woman, wearing a soiled housecoat, came to the door, and opened it slightly. She looked down, and saw the corsage Calman was carrying, and she turned crimson with embarrassment. She opened the door a little wider, and Calman stepped into the alcove, but the woman stopped him there.

"I'm here to pick up Stella," he said with some hesitation. He sensed something was wrong. The woman fumbled with her words.

"Stella is not home. She went out to a movie with her cousin a half hour ago. "But I confirmed our date last night." "I know," she said, looking at him foolishly.

"Izzie," she called to her husband, "Come here for a minute."

An unkempt man, unshaved and uncombed, shuffled towards them, and stood behind his wife, and without removing his lit cigarette, growled, "Why does a smart boy like you want to go out with my daughter, the stupid cow?"

Without a further word spoken, Calman turned around and walked out the door, and down the stairs. When he reached the bottom he threw the corsage into the gutter.

Calman reflected on this incident, dredged up from the past as fresh as if it had happened yesterday. He began to think.

Why had he been rejected by this third rate broad? Was he simply a schlemiel, a loser… out of the running? Or was this girl, for all her shallowness, able to see something in his character to which he himself was oblivious?

Now, years later, as his pace to nowhere was quickening, he began to understand something about his nature. Intellectual snobbery! A Faustus! That was it! Stella was fearful she would be humbled by his display of superior intellect. She would be unable to stand up to him, to his sense of entitlement.

My God. She was more honest than me.

Now, years later, there was the Saunders incident. Why had Vincent lied to him? Why had he led him on? Vincent, the articulate, debonair, self-assured, know-it-all, after all, felt threatened by Calman, and Calman pondered.

Do I set myself up, only to be let down?

Calman's thoughts turned to Ruth. He was in love with her. He had been certain she was also in love with him. Both of them were ready for marriage. After the weekend, he would pick her up at the depot, and drive her home, and she would probably shake his hand good-bye. Unwed, he already felt cuckolded.

Calman returned home, and phoned Marie Dunn. He would be able to talk to her about his predicament. Maybe he'd also get laid.

"Hello!" came her cheerful voice over the wire.

"Hello, Marie!"

"Cal, how are you? Has your car rolled down any more hills?"

"No! I thought I'd give it another chance," he bantered. "If you're free tomorrow evening I'd like to see you. I'll take you to a quaint French restaurant."

Marie detected an urgency in his voice. "Is there anything wrong Cal? Can we discuss it on the phone?"

"No, no," he said a little strained, "I just thought…" his voice trailed away, as she interrupted.

"Cal, I'm going to be married."

CHAPTER XV

Calman parked his car, and walked towards Union Station, one of the oldest and most important of Toronto's landmarks; it constituted the busiest train terminus in Canada. He had glanced at the board noting arrivals and departures, and saw that the Philadelphia train was expected to arrive on time. He took a seat on one of the hard wooden benches, and waited. He wondered, with some trepidation, what Ruth would have to tell him.

The grating of the wheels, and the shrill whistle of the trains as they lumbered out of the station, was all that was needed to send Calman on an introspective journey of his own.

He recalled his first train ride. He was only eight, and his parents had made a last minute decision to send him off to camp. But it was too late to catch the bus filled with boys, laughing and squealing, and scrubbed clean. So they rushed Calman to the train station where his father bought him a ticket, and they waited for the train's arrival.

"What did the ticket cost?" his mother asked.

"Three dollars and fifty cents," his father replied indifferently.

"It's too much," she answered him. He ignored her, and she continued, "Do you realize that between the camp, and the transportation and clothes, and spending money for Calman, it amounts to a full month's wages?"

After a few minutes of expectant silence, she repeated, "Do you hear what I'm saying – a full month's wages."

"We made the decision together. You're making the boy feel uncomfortable."

Calman felt, not only uncomfortable, but also guilty, and he was fearful. He had never before been separated from his family. The morning was misty, and as the train locomotive plunged through the fog and smoke, Calman connected it with a huge monster, a dragon that would devour him, and a great fright took hold of him.

"I don't want to go," he fretted. "You have to go," his mother scolded him, "It's already paid for."

"What's the matter, Cal?" His father's voice was reassuring.

"It's too expensive. I know they'll return the money."

The parents exchanged knowing glances.

"Look here, Cal," his father said reassuringly, "Don't worry about the cost. Besides, all your friends will be here, and most of them come from families worse off than us."

Calman, of course, did not understand the meaning of a depression.

They walked to the platform, and Mr. Mencher approached the porter, spoke to him for a few moments and then nodded at Calman. He then put something into the porter's hand, and, patting Calman on the shoulder, slowly started to walk away. Mother hugged him and kissed him on the cheek.

"Now, obey the counsellors, and don't get into any fights."

"OK., OK."

Calman was left alone with the porter. He lifted him onto the train, as a voice resounded through the loudspeakers, "All Aboard." The porter led the frightened boy to his seat, and deposited his luggage. "Say! How would you like a chocolate bar?"

Now another voice sounded over the loudspeakers, at Union Station, which aroused Calman from his reverie, announcing the arrival of the train from Philadelphia. Calman's rumination ceased as he stood and began walking towards the arrival platform.

They saw each other simultaneously. He waved, and her face broke into a radiant smile. And in that moment, he experienced an intuitive insight, an epiphany. He realized that he had won the race, ahead of all his married friends. The clouds had lifted, and he went to embrace his bride. She dropped the heavy suitcase and ran into his arms.

"Oh Cal, I love you! I love you, I love you!"

She clung to his arm as they walked back to retrieve her suitcase. He lifted it, and carried it to the car. Once they were in the car, they embraced again, and they kissed passionately, until horns started honking around them. One car slowed down and as it passed them the driver yelled at them:

"Hey buddy, you're holding up traffic. Save it for dessert."

As they started to drive, Calman asked her, "Did you have a pleasant trip home?"

"I was worried all the way," she replied, "that you might not be here."

They drove on in silence, until finally, as they were approaching her home, Calman asked, "Did you find what you went for?"

"What I went for?" She repeated his question.

"Closure!" he said.

"Closure! Oh, yes! Absolutely!"

Calman's face relaxed into a smile, and he took her into his arms, and kissed her. He thought he heard her mutter as she mellowed blissfully in his embrace, "This is closure."

CHAPTER XVI

Three years had passed since Calman had performed the Chaplin duck walk at the home of Dr. Carole Williston, somewhere on the Hamilton Mountain. He had told Ruth of the incident, and they had enjoyed a good chuckle over it.

They were married on a sunny Sunday, two months after Ruth's return from Philadelphia. Her father, Reb Fischel, insisted that Calman join him at the synagogue early in the morning on the day of the wedding. Together they davened – prayed – as they wound the phylacteries seven times around their left arms, and once on their foreheads.

Ruth had told him, "You don't have to go." But Calman wanted to humour the old man. When he got there, and went through the ancient Hebrew ritual, he felt a warm glow of comfort, as it brought back memories of his grandfather with whom he used to pray as a boy.

During the three years, they had purchased a house situated on a large lot in a new suburban development located in Willowdale, at Toronto's north-central quadrant. The front of the house was bounded by a large garden, where Ruth had planted with a variety of flowers – roses, tulips, daisies, and numerous shrubs. And there were four Willow trees.

The rear of the house opened up to a large yard, nearly half an acre, and it was Calman's job to see to it that it was mowed, and cleansed of dog pooh. They had acquired a black Labrador that they called Liquorice. They were also expecting their first child.

Calman had moved into larger offices, on Yonge Street near Sheppard Avenue, within walking distance from his home. Sometimes, he would return to the old haunt, and park his car at Charlie Tepper's, and the two would lunch together at the delicatessen. His practice had grown, due in large measure to recommendations from his bank manager, Dick Norris, his client Abe Schnier, and Charlie Tepper. He had acquired a modest staff, including an articling student, and a secretary who also served as a receptionist.

Carole Williston's family had also grown. She was now a mother of two, and was expecting a third child. Calman's high regard for Carole had dwindled since she had married Ken. He felt that she had betrayed herself, and her family, by marrying intellectually so far beneath her. Someday, he thought, she would regret her folly. But for the present, she was too busy having babies. And she was still oblivious to the tensions between her husband, and Calman. One day, when Calman was consulting with her at her home, the elderly Mrs. Waitzer walked in.

"Oh, hello Mr. Mencher," she said, obviously happy to see him. He stood up,

"Hello, Mrs. Waitzer. It's nice to see you again."

At that moment Ken poked his head in, and a frown covered the elderly lady's face. Her dislike for her son-in-law was transparent.

"Excuse me," Ken said, and withdrew, shutting the door.

Why is this guy always around? Doesn't he work anymore? Has he lost his flying license?

But this was no concern of Calman's. Nor, for that matter, were Carole's personal affairs. He did not class her amongst his friends. She was simply a client, and he billed her according to the time he spent on her work, on an hourly basis. Calman had learned how to handle Ken – simply by regaling him with jokes. But Calman was also perceptive enough to see that Kenneth was threatened by his presence, and that much anger simmered behind the laughter.

Ken's insecurity was further compounded by the fact that Carole was firmly established as the family matriarch. She was the family intellectual, as well as the practical one. It was she who prepared the meals, and attended to the children's needs, she who handled the banking and paid the bills, and she who arranged their social, and cultural life. Ken was left out of all family decision-making.

A useless appurtenance.

Observing the manner in which Carole and Kenneth functioned together, Calman was reminded of existence in shtetles, the Jewish communities in Russia and Poland during the eighteenth and nineteenth centuries. The husbands spent their days studying Talmud at the Jewish seminary, and arguing over minute and esoteric points, while their wives managed the household. They also did all the baking and cooking, took care of the children, milked the cows and worked the fields, and kept the family clothed. And they handled all money matters.

Kenneth was also immersed in reading – comic books.

CHAPTER XVII

Lester Michaels had walked into Charlie's office, unannounced, and as Calman arrived, Charlie was admonishing him, "Next time you want to see me, call for an appointment. I don't like people barging in on me. I just can't drop everything because you think you need a legal opinion."

Charlie looked up, and saw Calman waiting patiently. "Hello Cal!"

Calman sniffed the air. "Aha! I see we're having corned beef, and cabbage, for lunch." He greeted Lester: "Hello Les."

"Do you two know each other? Charlie asked.

"Now, don't you remember, Charlie? I introduced you. Lester happens to be my client too."

"No wonder I'm broke," Les muttered.

When Calman had first met Lester, he was Leo Muskovitz, and he was a budding director of plays. As he had become more prominent, Calman had suggested that he change his name to something a little more Anglo-Saxonish, Hollywoodish. Now Les was being offered a movie contract, his first, and he wanted Charlie to look it over.

Charlie asked Lester, "Do you want to join Cal and me for lunch? We're going next door. Bring the agreement with you and I'll read it during lunch."

"Sure! I guess, if you'll be eating lunch on my time, there will be no charge."

"O.K. But you'll have to pay for the lunch."

The three of them walked next door to the delicatessen. As they were being seated, Charlie remarked to Lester, "I saw your production of Hamlet. My wife enjoyed it very much. She'd like to meet you."

"I didn't produce Hamlet. I directed the play." "Oh!" Charlie sallied back, "I thought you wrote it."

Calman and Lester each ordered a corn beef on rye, and Charlie had a pastrami. While they were waiting for the food, Charlie asked Lester if he had brought the contract with him. Lester withdrew the folded agreement from his breast pocket, and handed it to Charlie, who began reading it.

"Hmm!" he said playfully, "You are named as the party of the second part. They are the party of the first part. I object."

"Please, just read the contract. If you don't mind, I'll do my own editorializing." Charlie read on for a couple of minutes. Then, taking off his glasses he looked a little askance at Lester.

"Les, have you read this document carefully?"

"Of course I have. What do you think? Should I sign it?" "Well now, they're willing to pay you a lot of money. And they want you to direct Margaret Ashley. All this is to the good. But have you really read this contract?"

"Yes, of course."

"Then you must be aware that there are some serious limitations. One of them is the imposition of huge penalties if you don't finish on time, regardless of the reason."

"What sort of reasons?"

"Any! By way of example, you become ill and can't continue, the star dies or becomes incapacitated, an Act of God. I think they're being unreasonable."

"I "I know. But this is a chance of a lifetime."

"Don't worry. I won't kill the deal for you. Let me make some changes, and we'll wire it to them for consideration. Come back to my office, after lunch, and we'll work on it."

While they were waiting for their sandwiches, someone caught Lester's attention, and a frown crossed his face. The others looked up, and there, as large as life, stood the famous critic, Howard Kravitz, complete with his icon – a heavy cane with a handle made of a wart hog tusk, which immediately drew Calman's interest. Kravitz had written a review of Lester Michael's direction of the Ionesco play *Rhinoceros*, in which he had demolished Lester.

Kravitz beamed a smile at Lester. "Hello, Lester," he said, offering to shake hands. "Get away from me, you bastard," Lester growled.

"Come on now, Les, don't be childish. If you can't take criticism you should not be in the performing arts."

Lester turned away from him, and addressing Charlie and Calman, asked, "Do you smell something rotten?"

"You mean in the State of Denmark?" Calman quipped. Lester ignored the reference to Hamlet, and Kravitz took a seat at their table. He looked at Charlie.

"Haven't we met?" he asked Charlie.

"I go to many plays, and I've never missed a concert. I've often seen you sitting near the back row, taking notes. Why don't you sit near the front?"

"That's so I can make a quick exit if the play is lousy," he answered, glancing sideways at Les.

Calman broke up the heavy silence.

"Mr. Kravitz, I've been admiring your cane. Would you consider selling it?"

"This cane was given to me by Sir Lawrence Olivier a couple of years ago when I was in London. He was performing at the Royal Vic. I've got a bad leg now, and I cannot get around without it. No it's not for sale."

The food arrived, and they became engrossed in their sandwiches. Charlie bit into his pastrami with gusto, and called out to the waiter, "Harry, where are the pickles?

"Coming up!" Harry called back.

Kravitz saw that Lester was somewhat less belligerent, now that his mouth was full, and he took advantage of the opportunity to placate him.

"After all we're friends, Les. I don't have to remind you that I usually give you a good review, because usually your work has the stamp of excellence. But sometimes, your direction lags. In the case of the Ionesco play, I felt that it fell below your high standard, and when that occurs, you need to be reminded. That's my job."

"My name to you is Lester, or Mr. Michaels, not Les."

Fine, Mr. Michaels, but please remember that I also have my standards."

Lester said, "Huh!" And Calman spoke up.

"Mr. Kravitz, I don't care for Ionesco, personally. I think Theatre of the Absurd lacks form, and besides, it's boring."

Kravitz interrupted: "You sound like my accountant."

Calman was shocked by the unexpected perception of the man, and Charlie laughed, and slapped his thighs. Even Les smiled. When the bemusement, caused by Kravitz' unintended witticism settled Calman continued, "However, my wife admires the man. So we went to see the play. I must have missed your review. Can you tell us what you wrote about the play?"

"When you say it lacks form, I assume you mean that it lacks structure," Kravitz replied. "That's precisely why it's absurd. But the absurdity also has a message for us."

"Yes, I know," said Calman, "But that appeals mostly to the intellectual know-it-all. I think a good play should have a plot and tell a good story."

"No," said the great critic. "A good play should reveal a universal theme. The play *Rhinoceros* manifests the absurdity of life, of the human condition. The fact that nearly everyone in the cast is transformed into a rhinoceros, except for the hero, should not be taken literally.

"Then how should it be taken?"

"Metaphorically!"

"Yes, I think I do understand what you mean. The whole play, including the title, is sort of symbolic."

"That's very good! Mr. ahh…"

"Mencher!"

"Are you a writer, Mr. Mencher?"

"No, I'm an accountant."

A burst of laughter came from a number of patrons who had been listening to the discussion. Charlie slapped his thighs again, and nudged Lester. This time Kravitz grinned too. But he was on a run, so he continued.

"Yes! Ionesco's message is really quite simple. The concentration on order, and materialism, is stifling Western culture, and we have become a thick-skinned, selfish people. We go galloping around and trampling each other just like the rhinoceros. Mr. Michaels here simply missed the symbolism of the rhinoceros, and hence the production fell flat."

"Oh! Is that what I missed?" Lester sneered in the most sardonic tone he could muster. "And tell me, Mr. Distinguished Critic, exactly what did you miss?"

"What did I miss?" Kravitz snickered back. "Clarify that, please."

"All right! I will. The play ran for three successive nights – Thursday, Friday and Saturday. Your review appeared on Saturday. So you must have seen the play on Thursday, or Friday. Is that correct, Mr. Critic?"

"So what!" Kravitz acknowledged impatiently.

"So, when were you there – Thursday or Friday? On the other hand, perhaps you were not there at all, and you just sent down a substitute to fill in for you, say a young sophomore, such as, forgive me, your teen-aged daughter?"

Kravitz's face now turned scarlet.

Lester rose from his seat. "You son-of-a-bitch! You wrote a scathing criticism of my direction…"

Everyone in the restaurant had turned to stare at them, "and you did not even see the performance."

Lester slammed his fist onto the table, and the plates rattled. He stormed out of the restaurant. Kravitz got up, and hobbled after him. Calman looked at Charlie.

"That was some dramatic scene. I wonder if they rehearsed it."

"Yep," said Charlie. "Now there's an example piece of Theatre of the Absurd."

"Not quite absurd as you think, my friend," Calman quipped, "They left us to pay the bill."

CHAPTER XVIII

March, 1955, and construction crews were repairing the Queen Elizabeth Highway. Calman had to detour from his usual route to Dr. Williston's home. He became a little discombobulated when he tried to take a shortcut. He was relieved when he finally arrived, only half an hour late, for the meeting. *Carole would understand.* However, when Carole answered the door, Calman knew at once that something was wrong. She was polite, as always, but her usual cheerful disposition was not there

He tried to surmise what could have brought about this change.

Perhaps one of the babies is sick. No! It's not that. Could it be that she is vexed with me for being late? No! She is not like that. Perhaps she and Ken have quarreled. Yes! He knew instinctively that that was it. Now what did they quarrel about that left her in such a state? Could it be money? Possibly! Money is often at the root of marriage problems. But he discarded that theory. Could it have something to do with me?

It hit him square.

They must have quarreled because of me.

These thoughts passed through Calman's mind, not as sequential reasoning, but in a stream of intuition. The realization left him with a sinking feeling at the pit of his stomach.

Carole's words came stilted, "I guess I should have called to warn you about the road conditions."

"No problem," he said, trying to be cheerful. "It gave me a chance to explore your neighbourhood. It's charming."

Carole managed a weak smile.

"Before you leave, I'll give you directions on how to avoid the traffic congestion."

They had been standing in the vestibule, and she now turned and walked towards her office, beckoning him to follow. He noticed the cane in its stock, and he smiled as he recalled the time he had performed the Charlie Chaplin duck walk. She noticed the transitory incident, and they exchanged smiles.

But, as they entered the office, she half turned to him, and said apologetically, "I'm afraid I shall have to disappoint you today. I've been so busy with the practice, and with looking after the children" – there were three, and Calman detected that a fourth was on the way – "that I haven't found time to do the paper work."

"Don't worry," he assured her, "I'll take your vouchers and write up your books at my office."

Her voice almost rose to a cry.

"Oh, no! You mustn't do that. I'll write them up this evening."

Calman saw her eyes becoming moist. He also thought he saw a shadow lurking behind the door, listening.

"All right," he said kindly. "Let me know when you're ready."

She extended a limp hand.

Calman looked at his watch. It was four-thirty. Ruth was expecting him home, at six. There was no point in returning to the office. His visit with Dr. Williston had not been pleasant, and he was relieved to have escaped the tense atmosphere and now, away from that scene, he began to speculate on whether Carole had been beaten by Ken. He had never seen her so cowed, and he wondered whether he should call Mr. Wolfe and discuss the dilemma with him. He drove on with a sense of frustration. Moreover, traffic was congested, and this added to his distress. So he turned on the radio, listened to some music, and then the news. Somehow, he managed to arrive home just a few minutes after six.

Even before he opened the door, the delicious aroma of roast beef, gravy and hash brown potatoes assailed his nose, and his angst passed. Ruth was bent over the bassinette bathing baby Liz. She passed the soapy washcloth between her legs, and around her pink little bottom. Lizzie let out squeals of delight. She splashed the water, drenching Ruth's hair, face and dress.

"Whoosh," Ruth said as Calman entered the room, "Here's daddy."

Liz stared at the man who was interfering with the fun. She was unhappy, and started to pucker her face into a crying mode. But Calman joined the fun too, and soon had her cooing again, as he powdered her, fed her, and sang her to bed, and all the while, Bobo, the black spaniel, was getting under foot. Finally, Ruth and Calman settled down at the dinner table.

"Did you have a good day?" she enquired.

"Well," he drawled, "I lost an old client today, or, at least, I think I did."

"Oh! Who is the client?"

"Dr. Williston."

He attempted indifference.

"But I thought she liked you," Ruth said, in surprise. "Do you want to talk about it?"

"Well, you see, the explanation is really quite simple. It has nothing to do with fees, or service. The fact is that Carole's stud, Ken Hughes, is intimidated by me, and doesn't want me around."

"You are, of course, referring to her husband."

"Yeah!"

"Why do you call him her stud?"

"Why not! Because that's about all he's capable of, and…and…"

"And you don't like him?"

"It's mutual."

"And you show him up whenever you go to their home, don't you?"

"I think I show him *down*. I don't really visit their home. I go to Carole's office, which happens to be in their home."

"Why is it necessary to show him up…or down?"

"It's not necessary. He brings it on himself. He is somehow always present when we have our business meetings. I don't ask questions, but I do wonder when he works, that is, *if* he works. As for Carole, I think she is starved for stimulating conversation, and she draws me out whenever I'm with her. She wants to know what books I'm reading, what theatre we have seen, what concerts we've attended. Ken is, invariably, left out of these conversations, but that's his own doing, not mine."

"Why can't he be included?"

"He's not at all interested. He just walks out of the room."

"Doesn't he read?"

"Yes, comic books."

"Well, Carole seems to be an intelligent woman. Isn't she aware of what's going on?"

"Yes, you're right. She's a very bright woman. But, as for being aware, she hadn't the faintest notion until today. She was so obsessed with the guy that she was oblivious to the tension between the two of us."

"What do you mean 'obsessed'? Isn't she in love with her husband?"

"No doubt she *was* in love when they got married."

"Perhaps it was only infatuation."

"Perhaps. But, frankly, I think the honeymoon is over. The love part or the infatuation has worn off. Sooner or later, a blow-up had to occur. I think he may have even beaten her."

"Cal, that is very serious. If you think he's beaten her, we should call the police. Did you notice any bruises on her?"

"No, I didn't. But I do know that she'd been crying just before I got there. I think he'd been intimidating her."

"Yes! One can be abused mentally, as well as physically."

There was a long pause while Ruth removed the plates.

"Delicious meal," Calman opined.

She returned in a moment, placing his favourite dessert, blueberry pie, down on the table in front of him. The pie was freshly made, and was still warm and loose, with a starchy crust. He took hold of her hand, and kissed it. He dug his fork into the pie, and tasted it.

"Umm! Scrumptious!" Her lips brushed his cheek, and she said in her quiet way:

"It seems to me that, having lost her father years ago, she is still looking for him. Her husband, Kenneth, obviously cannot fill this role, so you are the substitute for the lost father. That's why you are important to her. I'm sure, from what you say, that her husband wants you out of the picture. He cannot compete with her father. This is why she's in distress. Perhaps you should simply resign. How important is she as a client?"

"She's not too important. I don't earn a great fee from her. The thing that upsets me is that I've never lost a client before."

"Well," Ruth comforted him, "You haven't lost her yet. It is the uncertainty that is causing your anxiety."

The phone rang at 8 p.m. Ruth lifted the receiver. After listening for a few moments, Calman heard her say, "Just a moment please. I'll get him."

She came quietly into the den where Calman was reading the late edition of the *Tely*, and said softly, almost solicitously, "I think it's Dr. Williston."

Calman's confidence had been bolstered by his talk with Ruth, and now he spoke firmly into the phone, even allowing a tinge of annoyance to enter his voice. Carole's voice, still demure, but muted, floated across the wire.

"Hello Calman; it's Carole Williston."

"Yes, I know," he retorted abruptly.

She was agitated, he could tell, and she spoke with hesitation, measuring each rehearsed word.

"As you know, Calman, I am carrying a heavy load, what with taking care of the household, looking after the children, and conducting a full-time practice."

There was an expectant silence from Calman.

Get to the point, he thought.

She continued nervously, stumbling over her words.

"I have therefore decided to join up with two colleagues who practice in my area. As a result, I will be able to reduce my office hours considerably."

She paused, and then in a half sob said, "Calman, my new partners insist that we engage their accountants."

Calman wanted to say: *That's all right. I was going to resign, anyway, because I can't stand that meddling nincompoop that you call husband. What are you waiting for? Why don't you toss the prick out on his ear?"*

But he felt sorry for her, and instead said this, "That's all right Carole, don't worry over it. I have some of your journals and other records in my office. I will have them packaged, and returned to you tomorrow."

"Calman, please send me your bill for today's visit. It will be paid promptly."

He noticed that she was using his full name instead of the abbreviated, familiar, Cal. A strained silence followed, and then she said, "You must be quite vexed with me."

But he was now in good spirits; relieved at having ended the uncertainty he had felt about this client for so long.

He would have liked to have said: *Your mother will be disgusted by your decision."*

But instead he replied, trying to suppress his newfound cheerfulness, "I, too, have changed dentists, doctors and lawyers. That's one of the hazards of being a professional."

"Thank you, thanks very much, Calman, for everything you've done for me, and for being so understanding."

She hung up and went back to weeping, and to her husband's cavil, "You should have fired that Jew bastard a long time ago."

In the Mencher home, Ruth said, "Well done."

CHAPTER XIX

April 1975. Twenty years had gone by. In a wink, seven thousand, three hundred days had passed…eighty seasons had come and gone. Each season marked a turn of events by which Calman could measure his personal growth.

In the early fifties, Ruth had introduced Calman to Allan and Jacqueline Steiner. Allan was dean of social work at the University of Toronto, but for three years running, during the summer vacations, he had run an art school in the Caledonian Hills. Ruth would spend a month there with the children, and her natural artistic talent bloomed. She painted scenes of nature, and of still life.

Calman took long weekends, leaving on Thursday evenings and returning on Mondays, but he lacked the talent, or even the will, to paint. One morning, however, as he was having his breakfast on the terrace, a little boy came running up to his mother crying out, "Mommy, Mommy, come see. There's a bare-naked lady."

Calman finished his coffee, stood up, and then, affecting nonchalance, strolled in the direction from which the child had come. He soon encountered a group drawing a live model, who was a beautiful woman, and he guessed her to be in her thirties. The art teacher noticed Calman hanging around and told him to stop loitering.

"You'll find nothing lurid here. So either leave, or join the class." He enrolled in the class.

It was this exposure to art that fired in Ruth a desire to paint, and in Calman, an interest in art. This newfound interest brought them into contact with prominent artists and their families. They also started to acquire art. Their introduction to the world of collecting was through a circle of elite Canadian landscape artists known as the 'Group of Seven.' The first painting they acquired was a Franklin Carmichael, a gift from their friends, the Muellers. Little did they or the Muellers realize the value of the painting at the time! The next piece was an A. Y. Jackson, purchased at an auction, for eighteen hundred dollars.

"Do you think we can afford it?" Ruth asked, beaming with happiness.

"We'll have to trim the budget, I guess," he replied, happy to see her so pleased with the new acquisition.

When the new McMichael Art Gallery opened, in 1966, with its impressive collection of the Group of Seven paintings, Ruth and Calman were among the first in the line-up to view the famous Canadian art exhibit.

The Menchers were invited to a dinner party in Bracebridge, a scenic town in northern Ontario, where several of the Group of Seven artists had resided at one time. The month was August. The party was being held at the Charlson's summer home, one of Calman's clients. Seated next to Calman was a young woman, not more than thirty, who seemed to know a great deal about the Group of Seven.

"Are you a famous artist?" Calman asked her.

"Well, I do paint, but I'm not famous."

"How do you come to have so much knowledge about the Group of Seven?"

"My father was a member of the Group." Calman was startled, and sat upright. "Who is your father?"

"Was! He was Frank – that is – Franz Johnson." Calman raked his memory. He reflected: *Not as famous as Tom Thomson, but then who is, nor Arthur Lismer, but still an important Canadian artist.*

As dessert was being served he asked her, "Do you have much of your father's work?"

"Some! Much of it hangs in the McMichael Art Gallery. But my mother has the best of his work."

"Your mother is still living? And without waiting for a reply he asked, "How old would she be?"

"Ninety-three years old, and she's still spry."

"Listen, do you think your mother would accept a visitor?"

"She loves to entertain visitors. Why don't you, and Mrs. Mencher come by tomorrow morning?"

On the following morning, after they had breakfasted with their hosts, Calman and Ruth set out for the home of Mrs. Johnson. It was hidden in a forest, and they could never have found it without the detailed instructions, and map which had been so painstakingly drawn for them by Eilene Charlson. The walls of the home were at least fourteen feet in height, leading into a spectacular vaulted ceiling. The back walls of the house were made of glass, a double-glazed thermo pane. The rear of the cottage hung in a space over an escarpment, looking down into a gorge at Lake Muskoka, and one could see the great jack pines, which the Group of Seven had made famous in their paintings.

As they entered the home, even before Mrs. Johnson could greet them, Ruth noticed a large oil hanging on the north wall, which caught and held her attention.

The old lady seemed frail, but she was gracious and full of spirit.

"Take all the time you want," she said, and offered her visitors pastries, cheeses and coffee. Calman accepted a cracker, and cheese. Ruth declined to partake, and turned her attention again to the painting on the wall.

It was titled *Farewell*, and it depicted a scene of native Indians on land waving goodbye to several missionaries who were departing in a canoe for the mainland. Except for a few cumulous clouds, the sky was clear, serene blue. The grass was sparse, and showed brown patches. Obviously, it was late autumn.

Ruth turned to Mrs. Johnson. "Ohh, dear! I love this painting."

"It's my favourite too," the old lady retorted.

"Would you be willing to sell it?"

"My dear," the ancient lady replied. "I will sell you any of my other paintings. But I cannot part with this one. It was painted in October 1921, during our honeymoon, on a hill overlooking the Albany River. I sat beside my husband as he painted, and I can remember every brush stroke."

There was a stillness as Ruth walked the room, stopping to examine the different exhibits. Calman followed with hands clasped behind his back.

Mrs. Johnson then announced proudly, "My husband also painted abstracts."

"I didn't know that," said Ruth. "I thought that the Group of Seven were renowned for their landscapes. Did the other members of the Group also paint abstracts?"

"I really can't say."

She disappeared quickly into one of the other rooms. Within moments, she was back in the room carrying an oil canvas in frame, the picture facing Ruth and Calman. It was eighteen inches wide, and thirty inches in height. It was a busy painting, and it was also asymmetrical, with oranges, yellows, green and blues popping, and jumping up, all over the canvass in little swirls.

"I think your husband was painting music, Mrs. Johnson," Ruth exclaimed. The old lady stopped in her tracks. There was a deadly silence.

"Did he enjoy modern music?" Ruth asked the astonished woman. "I believe I see Stravinsky's Rites of Spring."

Mrs. Johnson turned pale, and then started to weep. Her daughter, who had kept in the background, came running over, and helped her mother to a chair.

"Are you all right, mother?"

Ruth and Calman became alarmed, and they rushed to her side.

"Perhaps we should call a doctor," Calman volunteered. But Mrs. Johnson was starting to recover, and the colour, which had drained from her face, was returning to her cheeks. Ever so slowly, she now turned the painting over, and there on the back was written very legibly the words: *Stravinsky's Rites of Spring. – Franz Johnson.* Everyone, including Ruth, was wonderstruck. It took a few minutes for them to recover, and then Mrs. Johnson said to Ruth, "My dear Ruth, this painting shall be yours."

Calman interceded. "No, Mrs. Johnson, we cannot accept such a gift."

Ruth added, "You see, we really know very little about abstract art. My guess, after all, was only a guess, a coincidence, and nothing more. However, the piece we really like is your husband's early work *Farewell.*"

"Then you shall have it."

Calman drew the daughter aside. He whispered to her, "I don't think your mother really wants to part with that painting. If we take it, she may be sorry afterwards. She will miss it."

"No!" she replied. "You don't know my mother. When she makes up her mind, she's unshakable.

Calman turned to the old lady, who was still sitting in the wicker chair holding the *Rite of Spring* painting, and said to her, "Mrs. Johnson, I don't think you should part with this painting."

She stopped him. "And who, young man, do you think you are to come into my house and tell me what to do with my art? I have made a decision.

The painting, *Farewell*, is going with Ruth. She and I have already decided on that, haven't we Ruth?"

Ruth remained stupefied, while the daughter smiled knowingly. The old lady turned to Ruth.

"You see, my dear, I don't have much time, and I want his painting to have a good home. I believe I have found the person who will provide that home. However, I should like to make one stipulation – that you do not sell the painting during my lifetime."

Ruth bent down, and embraced Mrs. Johnson, as tears welled up in both their eyes. Calman turned to the daughter, and drew her aside. "What do you estimate to be the value of the painting?"

"Ohh! I don't know. Say, perhaps five thousand dollars. But I think my mother intends it as a gift for your wife."

"No! That is not negotiable. How about ten thousand?"

On the way home Ruth said wistfully, "I feel that we should not have taken the painting."

Calman replied, "Once this woman makes up her mind she's unshakable. There's no arguing with her."

CHAPTER XX

In the mid-fifties, before the Hungarian revolution, Calman met the Fass and Stern families, elegant and refined people, who had once belonged to Hungary's Jewish elite, but who had become victims, first of the Nazi regime, and then of the harsh Communist occupation. They had lost their families, and most of their possessions, but their dignity and culture had remained intact. Calman had learned a great lesson from them – that life is worth living, and that it is possible to survive under the most adverse condition.

He also met the Baron and Baroness de Szasz, two people as dissimilar as night was from day. They, too, had emigrated from Hungary to Canada, and had settled in Toronto. They were aristocrats, born and bred, and the Baron had great difficulty adjusting to the middle-class, English-speaking lifestyle.

The Baron was a large, formidable man, with square jowls, a head of wavy black hair and deep hirsute eyebrows. His voice was deep, gruff and heavy – heavy with the Hungarian accent, rolling his rrrs. He referred to Calman Mencher as *Menchairrr.*

He had once owned sugar beet fields in Czechoslovakia, and his demeanour and gait, suggested a man on horseback, whip in hand, riding amongst the peasant workers. Calman's mind, operating freely, made the association between the Baron and the Black Knight from the gothic novel, *Ivanhoe*, by the eighteenth-century writer, Sir Walter Scott. In Canada, the Baron's imperious disposition led him into trouble. Canadians were not intimidated by his insolent manner. Even his own countryman regarded him as pompous, and as a relic of the past.

The Baroness, by contrast, was a petite woman, graceful and elegant, but subdued, or so it seemed, in contrast with her boisterous husband. But she had his number, and without doubt, she controlled the household in a quiet way. She was smart, and capable, and soon after their arrival in Canada, she realized that there were great opportunities in real estate.

She consulted with Calman without her husband's knowledge, and together they found a twenty-four-unit apartment building on which she decided to make an offer. She made the mistake, however, of telling the Baron of her plans to purchase the property, and he forbade her to have anything to do with such lower, middle class, nouveau riche enterprises.

Instead, he found a business more to his liking, and more suitable to his autocratic mien. He bought acres of timberland, and began a business of cutting, and logging, timber. Here, he could again walk about or ride his horse, whip in hand, ordering and directing the loggers, and showing his dominance.

There came a day when the Baron met a Frenchman from Quebec, Dominic Barrager, who owned the local sawmill. De Szasz took his new acquaintance to the local pub, and there, through a piece of brilliant maneuvering, he managed to persuade Barrager to sign a contract giving the Baron the exclusive use of Barrager's plant, thus guaranteeing the processing of all his timber output through the sawmill. He also tied up Barrager, in an employment contract that required him to manage the sawmill.

But there were two things the Baron had not reckoned with. The first was that the mill was old and obsolete, and he would have to spend large sums to rebuild, and re-equip the plant. The second problem was that he failed to take into account the fact that Monsieur Barrager was a heavy tipster, never without his bottle of Seagram's whisky.

On a cold February day, Calman paid a visit to the de Szasz home, where the financial records were maintained. During the previous night, there had been a heavy snowfall, and he had to tread through nearly four feet of snow to get to the de Szasz entranceway from the street. He was admitted, by the Baroness herself, and was surprised to discover that their home was a modest house, 1930's vintage. The books and vouchers were laid out on the dining room table, waiting to be examined, and recorded by Calman. Though it was daytime, the outside was dark and dismal. But the Baron refused to turn on the lights.

Calman thought to himself: *This guy is cheap and he's got a mean streak.*

He started sorting out the vouchers and making journal entries. The Baron sat in a large wing chair, watching him. After a while Calman addressed the Baron.

"Excuse me, Sir, I see a number of cheques made payable to a Mr. D. Barrager, What did you buy from him?"

"I help him to fix his sawmill."

"I thought so. I've heard of this Barrager fellow who gets suckers to invest in his sawmill."

"What is dis suckers?" the Baron interrupted. He knew well enough what Calman meant.

"Investors," Calman said in a sarcastic tone. "And I calculate that you have already given him seventy-eight thousand dollars, but…" the Baron interrupted him, "Dis is not yourrr business." He spoke with a deep growling 'rrr'. Calman noticed that the Baroness was standing discreetly by the door. He answered, "I'm sorry sir, but…"

The Baron intruded again with an outburst, "Sorrry! Vat is dis sorrry? I hear all de time you Canadians say you are sorry. For what reason you are all de time sorrry?"

"It's only an expression. If you don't mind, now, I should like to continue. I see that you have not been generating any income, and that you have no sales from the sawing operation. Now, I have some doubts about this Barrager…"

The Baron went into a rage. "I say dis is not yourrr business." And, reverting to a guttural German, spouted out, *"Du bist der buch-halter!"*

Calman saw the poor lady cringing in the doorway, trying to beckon him to contain his temper, but he could not help her. Instinct took hold of him. He rose from his chair, and stood facing the Baron.

"Ich bin nicht kein buch-macher!" Calman barked. "I am a Chartered Accountant, and none of my clients has ever gone bankrupt, and none will go bankrupt…not on my watch. I resign!"

He picked up his briefcase, shoved in some papers, closed it, and strode to the vestibule, where he put on his galoshes, hat and coat, while the Baroness, wringing her hands, prevailed on him not to leave. But he left. He trudged through the snow back to his car; having made a mental note of the look of consternation that had crossed the Baron's face at the mention of the word 'bankrupt'."

Calman was about to enter his car, when he felt a hand on his shoulder. The Baron had come running after him through the snow in his slippers. One slipper had fallen off and he bent to look for it in the snow. He retrieved it, and turning to Calman, said in a conciliatory voice, "Menchairr, where you arrre going?"

Calman would have liked to have answered: *none of your business.* But the man had humbled himself, and so he replied instead, "I'm returning to my office."

"Please, Menchairr, don't go. Come back in."

"I'm sorry, I can't work with you. Why should I come back?"

"Because I like you."

"You like me?" Calman was shocked. "I don't understand. Why?"

"Because you arr simpatico."

Simpatico! This was the first time anyone had used this word to characterize Calman. He was flattered. He turned around, and followed de Szasz into the house. The Baroness was at the door, and greeted him with a wide smile. From that time on, Calman never again referred to deSzasz as the Baron or Baroness. They were, henceforth, called Mr. and Mrs. deSzasz.

It was getting dark, and as they returned to the dining room, Mr. de Szasz turned on the light. He then took out a bottle of brandy, and poured a shot for each of them.

"Your health!" said deSzasz and they both downed their drinks. DeSzasz began to laugh, and Calman looked at him quizzically.

"You know why I laugh?" he asked. "Because you say you are not a buchmacher. Ha! Ha! Ha! Buchmacher means bookie."

Calman smiled at his error. And after a while, de Szasz continued, "But you are right. Dis man Barrager is a drunk. And he is also a crook. Menchairr, tell me, what should I do?"

Calman now took command. "First," he said. "You must stop advancing him any money. Is that agreed?"

The older man nodded.

"Now, we will call your lawyer, and ask him to register a lien on the property for the amount you have advanced to him. Third, I suggest you put up your timberland for sale. This is not the right business for a gentleman like you. You should reconsider real estate."

By the time Calman was ready to leave, a mental weight had been lifted from the deSzaszs,' and thereafter they made no financial decisions without first consulting Calman. He had become their guru.

One day, nearly a year after the reconciliation between Calman and deSzasz, Ruth called Mrs. deSzasz and introduced herself, and invited them to dinner for the following Friday evening. Ruth decided to prepare a traditional Jewish Friday evening dinner. Her guess was the right one, and Calman's aristocratic clients were thrilled.

The dinner commenced with Ruth lighting the candles, and reciting the traditional benediction. The deSzaszs were all attention. Calman then recited the prayer over the bread, the Sabbath chala, and he sliced it, and passed the parts around. He then raised his wine goblet and chanted the blessing over the wine, and they all drank.

Mr. DeSzasz, wiped away a tear.

"I remember, when I was a boy, I used to watch my grandfather perform these rituals," he remembered. There was stunned silence, broken finally by his wife.

"It was a beautiful, and moving ceremony, Ruth and Cal. Thank you."

Ruth then served the traditional Sabbath meal – a scoop of liver paté, and another of chopped egg and onions, followed by consommé with matzo balls. The entrée consisted of roast beef, and chicken, with dark hash potatoes, cooked to perfection. And for dessert, stewed prunes followed by sponge cake and tea. During the evening the wine flowed as did the conversation. But no reference was made to the Baron's tearful outburst.

At the end of the evening, Elizabeth de Szasz said to Calman, "Dear Calman, I would like to see your wine cellar."

Calman was a little embarrassed. "Mrs. deSzasz," he started to reply… "Elizabeth," she interrupted. "All right, Elizabeth! But my wine collection is very modest."

"Show me," she could also be imperious. He led her into the basement and showed her his passable wine cooler. "Hmm! Just as I thought," she mused, "You are buying expensive wines and overpaying. Would you be free to meet me next Tuesday?"

Calman nodded.

"Good I am going to teach you how to buy good wines at reasonable prices, and I promise you Calman, by the time I am finished you will be a wine pundit."

The de Szasz family lived only a short distance from the Menchers, and they accepted Calman's offer to drive them home. When Calman arrived at their home, Mr. de Szasz asked him to wait for a few moments. He then went swiftly into the house and returned shortly carrying a cane.

"I notice Menchairr that you are a collector of canes," he said, handing Calman a cane with a shaft made of palmetto wood, containing a bone handle which had been carved into the face of a bulldog, and a ferrule made of bone. "Keep this cane. Let it be a reminder always. It was given to me by a Jewish friend the day before he was seized by the Nazis, and shot in the streets."

Calman never again saw the Baron de Szasz display a tear.

When Calman returned home Ruth had already cleared the table, and put away the dishes, and cutlery. He displayed the cane to her and gave her a brief account of its history.

"It will make a great addition to your collection," she commented.

During the night, Calman was restless. About three o'clock in the morning he awoke, and went down to the kitchen. Ruth found him there, reading and having a cup of tea, and joined him.

"Were you unable to sleep?" she asked him.

"I kept thinking of the Baron."

"I knew you would." she said. "There was a poignant moment, last evening, when he shed a tear as we were performing the Sabbath rites."

"Yes!" Calman answered. "They are Catholic, you know, and their children were raised as Catholic. But I believe that Jewish blood runs in his veins."

"But the Baroness is a Christian, and a true Hungarian aristocrat."

"Yes! You can see it in her character – to the manor born."

CHAPTER XXI

"Hey guys, this is my wife, Carole. Bring us a few beers, will ya hon?"

"Nice to meet ya doc."

"Hey, Ken! You did O.K. for yourself. And she's not a bad looker too."

"I'll see ya. And raise you two."

Carole's friend, Anne Brody, who was on the teaching staff at Sheridan College, had called her a few days earlier, to invite her out.

"We're a group of four girls, and we go out to dinner once a month, and then we go to the symphony. One of the girls had to cancel for Thursday evening, and so we have an extra symphony ticket. I thought you might care to join us. Please say you'll come."

Carole was now the mother of five children. She was preoccupied with her work, and with all the family responsibilities. There was not time for fun or relaxation. Ken was away, flying, three weeks out of four, and was of little help even when he was home for one week. She had hired a helper to be with the children while she was away, working at the clinic. But she insisted on making the meals herself and on putting the children to bed.

"I would love to join you and meet your friends. I'll see if I can get Ken to stay home with the children."

Carole returned home after a memorable evening with Anne and her friends. This was the first mental stimulation she had enjoyed since her last meeting with Calman Mencher.

She walked into her private office, the one retreat in the house where she could find a moment of peace and contemplation, only to find it occupied by a band of six drinking, smoking, poker-playing ruffians. Their host was Ken Hughes. She ran out, and went to the children's rooms, to make sure they were safe. Then she went into the kitchen, and sat down at the table, and started to cry.

After a few minutes, she dried her eyes, and started to clean up the mess which she had found in the kitchen. She washed the dishes, and then dried them (they did not have a dishwasher yet.) She returned the dishes to their place in the cupboard. Then she cleaned the table of the crumbs, and other leavings, and straightened out the chairs. As she was leaving the kitchen to go to the bedroom, Kenneth walked in, hands in pockets.

"Hey! What's the matter with you?" he railed. "I asked you to bring us a few beers. Are you trying to gall me or something?" She had never seen him so odiously offensive, and didn't know what to make of it. But she knew that it boded no good, and a sinking feeling came over her. She managed to muster the courage to face him, and replied plaintively:

"You had no right to bring your friends into my private office, and to mess it up with your cigar smoke and beer. I won't tolerate that."

"YOU," he screamed at her, "You won't tolerate that? And who th' hell do you think you are? You know, this house is mine as much as yours."

She feared the argument would escalate to something physical, and wisely, made no reply. Instead, she walked out of the room. Ken's friends had already left, and she went back into her office, and began cleaning up. That night she slept in her office, and was not troubled again by her wanton husband. But sleep did not come easy. Much of the night she spent cogitating.

She thought first about the evening she had spent with Anna and her friends. She had not had such an enjoyable, and stimulating, evening for a long time. Ken would never take her out to dinner or even to a movie. She realized that her life was vacuous, that she was intellectually stilted.

How could I have allowed myself to get into this situation? Here I am saddled with five children.

She felt a pang of guilt.

No, that is not true. They're wonderful kids, and I love them dearly. And as for Ken, well, he is my husband. Do I love him? Not with the passion I once had for him. And he was certainly irksome last night. Well, as they say, 'if you can't fight them, join them.' I'll just have to learn to put up with his friends.

Carole awoke at seven o'clock in the morning. The children were getting up, and she made a treat for their breakfast – French toast. Then she dressed her first-born, Linda, who was six years old, and packed her with a lunch, for school. She played for a while with the younger children and dressed them; each was vying for her attention. She diapered the baby with the second oldest girl helping her, until the nanny arrived.

She slipped quietly into her bedroom, and selected the clothes she would wear for the day. Ken was sleeping soundly, and she left without waking him.

When Carole arrived at her office, it was already nine o'clock. Her first appointment was scheduled for ten. Edna, her nurse, opened the door. She saw Carole sitting at her desk, with elbows on the desk and her hands, cradling her chin and cheeks.

"Good morning, what's up doc?" she chortled. "Say, how about a coffee?"

"Thank you! I think I will."

"Mrs. Jameson will be here at ten o'clock. I'll settle her in number one. Is that O.K.?"

"Yes, that will be fine."

"How long will you be with her?"

"About two hours."

"Carole, is everything all right? You seem distracted."

"No, I'm fine."

"Are the children O.K.?"

"Yes! Thanks for enquiring."

Edna left to prepare operating room number one, and Carole remained alone in contemplation.

No, I do not have to take part in Ken's vulgar antics nor put up with his crude buddies in order to keep the peace.

She began to think about her marriage to Ken.

The only communication we have is in the bedroom, which reminds me, he doesn't believe in contraception. I will have to consult my doctor about a tubal ligation... Now, where was I? Oh, yes! What do I have in common with Ken? The children, of course! But he's away so much they don't even know him. I used to travel with him on some of his flights, but I haven't for the past six years.

She mulled over her dilemma for a while, and picked up her coffee cup, but the coffee had become cold and felt tasteless. She put down the cup, and pushed it away. Her thoughts went off in another direction.

What I need is a good friend to confide in. Anna might be the right person, but I've only just renewed our friendship, and I wouldn't want to impose my troubles on her. What I need is a professional adviser, a psychiatrist or a marriage counsellor.

Out of nowhere Calman suddenly crossed her mind. She hadn't thought of him for years. Now, she recalled that his wife was a marriage counsellor.

What was her name? Ruth! That's it! Ruth! I could call her. No, I can't. It would be so embarrassing.

The door opened, and Edna stuck her head in. She sensed that Carole was having some troubled thoughts.

"Is everything all right?"

Carole nodded.

"Mrs. Jameson is here. Shall I prep her in number one?"

Carole sighed, "Yes! Please do!"

As she was entering the operating room Carole had one last thought:

Yes, I think I'll have lunch with Edna across the street, and unload my troubled thoughts to her. She's a good listener.

CHAPTER XXII

On the morning of November 22nd, 1963, Calman Mencher was driving east on Highway 401 to see his client, Howard Chalmers, and he turned on his car radio. He caught the half-end of a sentence…"and was assassinated half an hour ago while driving in a motorcade in Dallas."

At about the same moment he glanced into the rear-view mirror, and noticed that cars were slowing down and pulling over to the side of the road. Then he noticed that cars ahead of him were doing likewise. Men and women were emerging from their cars with looks of astonishment.

Calman also pulled over and stopped his car, but remained listening to the radio.

The announcer continued, "We repeat: President John F. Kennedy, the thirty-fifth president of the United States has been mortally wounded."

The drivers who had stopped moved together, drawn by a magnet of fear and awe. They were gesticulating at one another, some wildly and crying, some in disbelief.

A man, dressed in a business suit, carrying his briefcase out of habit, addressed Calman, "I can't believe this has happened." He shook his head. "How could such an atrocity take place in this day and age?"

"It's impossible," cried a hysterical woman, "I refuse to believe that President Kennedy is dead."

Calman said, "It sounds like a Wellesian practical joke. Do any of you remember the stunt that Orson Welles pulled in his famous Martian landing back in 1938?"

They stood around for some fifteen minutes, and were joined by other motorists, a group of strangers suddenly galvanized by a force none had ever experienced before. Gradually, they dispersed, and the spell waned, each going sadly on their own way. Calman returned to his car, and continued on his way to Howard Chalmer's office.

Howard's secretary, Mabel, greeted him. "I've just brewed some fresh coffee. Would you care for a cup, Mr. Mencher?"

"Yes, thank you. Have you been listening to the news?"

Howard sauntered into the room, "What news is that, Cal? A new budget?"

"No," he said, "Quick, turn on the T.V."

"Which channel?"

"It doesn't matter…any channel."

Calman, Howard, and several of the office staff crowded into Howard's small office to watch the events unfold. Some stood, and some sat on the floor, with legs and ankles crossed. All watched incredulously as the camera switched from the greeting of the president and his wife, as their plane landed, to the smile of the president as they rode through the streets of Dallas, to the president slumped in his wife's arms, to the hospital.

Calman thought of a line from the Irish poet, William Butler Yeats, "Anarchy is loosed upon the world."

After a while, Howard dismissed the staff for the day.

"No work will be done here anyhow."

Calman returned to his home, where he and Ruth continued their vigil over their own T.V. set. The entire city, the entire country, the entire world was asking the same question, "How could this happen in a civilized society?"

"That's the wrong question," Calman sneered at the T.V. commentator.

Ruth raised her eyebrows. "Well, then, what's the right question?

"How could this *not* have happened in an uncivilized world?"

"This tragedy," she said, "will awaken people to the social malaise that pervades the world. Perhaps something good will come of it."

"But there's one thing I can tell you," he said sadly, "The world as we know it will never be the same."

"Look," said Calman, "It seems they've caught the culprit.

Ken Hughes was in the bathroom, shaving his three days' growth of beard. They wanted to see him at headquarters. Carole was ironing his trousers, and listening to the radio when the news of Kennedy's assassination was announced. She came rushing into the bathroom.

"Did you hear the news Ken? The president of the United States has just been assassinated."

"Damn it! I've just nicked myself."

"Oh! I'm sorry. I'll apply an antiseptic."

"No! Just get out of here," he shooed her away.

Ten minutes later, he emerged, picked up his freshly ironed trousers, and walked into the bedroom, where he completed dressing.

Shortly afterwards, he came down to breakfast attired in his captain's uniform. Carole waited on him, but did not say a word.

Ken broke the silence, "So they killed Kennedy, eh? Served him right, the son-of-a-bitch."

He looked at Carole to see her reaction. But she did not respond to his vituperation. "What's the matter with you? The cat's got your tongue?"

Ken finished his breakfast, wiped his mouth clean with his napkin, and walked towards the door.

"You know," he said, "he was a bloody Democrat."

He started walking towards his car, when she called out to him, "Have you forgotten your briefcase?"

She held it out to him. He walked back, took the briefcase from her, and walked sheepishly to his car. They did not exchange any further words.

CHAPTER XXIII

When Calman began courting Ruth in the early fifties, she introduced him to her friends, Joan and Norman Walters. Norman was a social worker, like Ruth. At the beginning of her career, he had been her supervisor, and it was he who had convinced her to do postgraduate studies at the University of Pennsylvania.

Joan was an associate professor in the English department at the University of Toronto. They were both intellectuals with leftist leanings. Calman himself had once had a flirtation with the left-wing movement. When he was sixteen, and in rebellion, he liked to think of himself as a Trotskyite, not because he had intellectual convictions, but because he had discovered that this would impress the girls.

Now, though Calman had long since outgrown his infatuation with left-wing politics, the two couples remained close friends. It was their mutual love of literature that brought them together, frequently at the fireplace in either home, over a brandy and a pipe. Norman and Calman were both pipe smokers.

One cold February evening in 1964, Ruth and Calman arrived at the Walters' home in a blinding snowstorm, for dinner and talk.

As they emerged from the car Calman remarked, "I told you we should have cancelled. We'll be lucky if we can get out of this snow bank later."

"Oh Cal!" Ruth admonished, "Where's your spirit of adventure?"

With those words, Calman lifted Ruth, and carried her through the deep snow to the very door of their friends' home. He nearly stumbled. "You're getting clumsy, mein lover," she laughed. "And you're getting heavy, mein sweetheart," he retorted.

Calman pushed the buzzer, and was still carrying Ruth, when Norman opened the door.

"Well! Well!" Norman announced to the other guests. "It's Sir Walter Raleigh."

Calman put Ruth down, and she said mockingly, "Sir Galahad."

The other guests, most of them academics, had already arrived, and were seated at the table. Norman circumnavigated the long rectangle table, and filled each glass with a red wine, and then raised his own glass.

"A toast to the late John F. Kennedy. History will judge him as the most attractive, as well as the most charismatic U. S. president, although not necessarily the best."

The contentious Thelma Morgan slammed her hand down on the table and confronted Norman.

"And just what is that supposed to mean?" Thelma was a querulous woman, and you could expect fireworks when she was a guest at a dinner party. Calman felt sorry for her husband, mild-tempered Peter, who usually sat back quietly and had little to say.

"Are you telling us he was the worst?"

"The worst…the best," said Norman, "These are only relative terms. "My little toast was merely to light up the fireworks."

Thelma didn't waste a moment, "Look at the great things he did. He brought youth to the White House, and revived the tradition of the salon, complete with poetry readings and concerts, yes, right into the seat of government. He injected life into a decadent Washington."

Calman broke in, and said with a straight face, "And he brought trysting at the White House to a high art."

There were a few chuckles, but for the most part his remark was ignored. Ruth, who was seated next to him, slapped his wrist and grinned.

Jean Haberman addressed Thelma, "Don't you mean that Jackie did all that?"

Ruth nudged Calman, "That's Jeanie Finkelstein. I haven't seen her since high school days. I'll go over later to say hello."

"It's the same thing," returned Thelma. "And together they brought a charm, and elegance, to the White House, and fashion also. For the first time in its history America had its own way to showcase its royalty."

Thelma was passionate. Ruth agreed, "That's true, he and Jacqueline turned Washington into the cultural capital of the world."

Norman responded, "Yes, but he also brought America to the brink of a nuclear war with Russia, and he got the U.S. involved in the Viet Nam war. Many American lives will go down the toilet in this war."

Thelma was particularly loquacious this evening, and she answered Norman, "John F. Kennedy played an important role, in fact, he was instrumental in bringing down the Berlin Wall. This will change the face of European society. What are you smirking at Max?"

"For the better I hope!" said Max Sugarman.

Calman saw that the argument could develop into a personal confrontation, so he changed the subject.

"I wonder who was behind the assassination."

Sam Lapedus, a dean of mathematics, a quiet and modest man, but with a keen analytical mind, observed, "It could have been anyone. Kennedy, during his short-lived incumbency, managed to accumulate an array of enemies. Take the Russians. There was no love lost between them, and the U.S. president. They could have enlisted this dupe, Lee Harvey Oswald, who after all, lived in Russia for a while and was an avowed Marxist."

"That's right," Max, added. "He was planning to renounce his American citizenship and become a Russian citizen."

"Well," the dean replied, "Maybe. But I don't think it was the Russians. They're too smart to rely on an unpredictable loner such as Oswald to carry out such a high level operation. Besides, despite the war in Viet Nam and the harsh words between the two sides, there were signs of an entente. Also the Russians were looking for American technology. No, I believe the Russians have too much to lose to have attempted to assassinate the president."

"What about Castro?" David Schnier asked. "Didn't Kennedy give his approval to the F.B.I. or the C.I.A. to have Castro assassinated? Doesn't that give Castro an excuse…not just an excuse, a moral right, to do the same to Kennedy? You know, to pre-empt him…quid pro quo?"

"It's not quite that simple," the professor replied. First of all, I'm not sure that Kennedy advocated killing the Cuban leader. These are just rumours after the fact. Assassination may have crossed his mind, but I believe he would have quickly ruled it out. It would have been a very dangerous strategy and he knew it, as did Castro. If the American public were to learn, as a fact, that Castro had sent assassins into the U.S. to murder a popular leader, Castro knows that the Americans would need no further pretext to bomb Cuba into extinction."

"No, I don't think it was Castro," Max said, "That would simply be tantamount to cutting off your nose to spite your face."

The professor smiled at him benignly, as if dismissing a student who had made an insipid point, "Something like that!"

"So where do you start looking for the culprits?" Thelma asked.

And Sam Lapedus replied again, "You have to start looking for motives."

"Who had a motive to kill the president?" Judith Frankel, a quiet, mousy little spinster who taught Russian at a small university, asked. "Do you think it might have been the Mafia? Haven't they been at odds with the Kennedys for some time?"

Sam Lapedus had now assumed an air of authority. He was in the classroom and held sway. The questions were being directed at him. He answered Judith.

"If I were in charge of the investigation, I would treat the Mafia as a prime suspect. There's this fellow, Jimmy Hoffa, you know, the head of the Teamsters, a crude chap who acts like a gang chieftain. I don't know whether he is Mafia or not, but he's had a hate on for the president for a long time. Bobby Kennedy wrote a book called *The Enemy Within*, in which he exposes the corruption in the Teamsters. Hoffa would not be sorry to see the president disappear."

Walters Myers, who was a professor of history at the University of Toronto, had been toying with his wine glass, and now drained it, and cleared his throat:

"It also could have been some disaffected derange lunatic. I would not be surprised if it turns out that this Lee Harvey Oswald acted on his own. But who knows? Let's hope that the Warren Commission can get to the bottom of this mystery."

"You know," said Norman, as he started to refill everyone's glass, "The world is bewildered, and shaken, by the assassination of one of the most popular presidents in the history of the United States. Walter, can you give us some historical perspective on this tragedy?"

"The fact that the president could be murdered right out in the open in view of millions of witnesses is, I believe, indicative of a profound malaise that is pervading our society today."

"But," said Norman, "This is not a new phenomenon. It happened to Caesar; it happened to the Austrian Duke Ferdinand, which precipitated World War I; and it happened to Lincoln."

"That is true! But there is a difference, you know. This is the age of technology. The T.V. has made the world into a global village, as one of my associates says, and hence everybody knows what's going on in everybody else's back yard. I am prepared to agree that corruption, bribery, and adulteration has been going on since the beginning of civilization, but there is something different about it today. The difference is that today, when a cataclysmic event takes place, everybody, everywhere knows about it the moment it occurs. It is the seeming increase in such terrifying events, brought about by either human indifference, or opportunism, that is turning society into cynics and anxious, dejected masses."

"With all respect Professor," Thelma spoke up again. "Don't you think you are overstating the case?"

"Well, just look at what is happening to the eco system. Better still, speak to any environmentalist today, and hear what he has to say. He will tell you that the physical world is beyond reclamation, and it is only a matter of time before the world deconstructs. Yes, yes indeed!" Walter was angry. "We are rushing heedlessly and inexorably to our bitter end."

"Walter, I've never heard you talk so passionately on any subject," said Norman, "Can I fill your glass?"

Walter waived him off, and instead took out his pipe, and tobacco, filled his pipe, tamped down the tobacco, and lit up. Then, more reflectively, he said:

"Imagine a man driving a car towards a wall, which is one hundred yards away, at a speed of one hundred and fifty miles per hour. When he is thirty yards from the wall, he suddenly realizes he is going to crash, and he slams on the brakes. Too late! Mankind is the driver in the seat, and the wall is the end of life. That is where mankind stands relative to the world ecology. Our forests are being denuded. We're robbing animal and bird life of their sanctuaries, and the damage being done to the eco system through the destruction of our forests is inestimable."

Ruth chimed in, "What about the pollution of our waters?"

"And that too," the professor re-joined.

Calman interjected, "You know, I have a client, whom I cannot name, who dumps acid waste into Lake Ontario."

Gert Rhineholt cut him off. "Does he realize that he's killing the fish in the lake, and poisoning our drinking water?"

"Of course he does! It so happens also that he's an intelligent man, and, would you believe it, philanthropic. He has received several warning letters from the provincial government requesting him to stop the dumping, but he ignores them."

"The bastard should be horsewhipped," Jack Rhineholt, Gert's, husband remarked.

"No," said Calman, "That's not the answer. Hundreds of other businessmen are doing the same. I've had several discussions with him about this problem, and he claims that if the government enforced its own anti-dumping laws against everyone, he would be compelled to comply. But this is one law that has no teeth. Don't blame the business that's trying to compete in the open market. It's the government that's to blame."

Walter joined in again.

"You've heard of oil spillages. Well, as the saying goes, 'You ain't heard nothin' yet'. Wait till the oceans become polluted. Fish by the millions will be destroyed."

"You're right," Murray Abrams spoke up. "Why do people have to shit where they eat?"

Addie Markson, sitting next to him, winced and edged away from him.

"What about the air?" asked the usually timid Marsha Levine.

"And that too," Walter added. "The air is being contaminated by fumes, and the more vehicles on the road, the worse it gets."

"So, would we be better off if we used diesel?" Marsha asked.

"No!" said Walter. "Same thing. They also give off air pollutants, and gases such as oxides of carbon, nitrogen and sulphur, and soot too, which affect the air we breathe, our crops and even our climate. Do you know what causes global warming? Too much carbon dioxide, and other gases trap the heat in the atmosphere.

"And what about all the testing of nuclear bombs that is going on?" Marsha asked.

"Do you think," Walter cried out. "That the fallout doesn't get swept through the atmosphere? Is it any wonder that cancer is growing to epidemic proportions? And this situation will only get worse. Big business is constantly searching for new markets, and so more and more cars, and other gas driven machines are filling the environment. Even the poor nations are consuming these products, and don't think for a moment that they don't have their eye on the nuclear intelligence of the West. It's only a matter of time."

Lisa Myers, Walter's wife admonished him. "Walter, this is not a lecture hall. Please, stop monopolizing the conversation, and let someone else speak."

"Sorry." he said, and stopped talking. He held up his glass, and Norman came over, and filled it up.

Calman, who was sitting next to him, joked with him. "A little thirsty this evening, Walt. Maybe you had better eat something."

Dr. Dorothy Caplan was a newcomer to the group. She was a visiting professor of philosophy, and was staying with the Myers.

"May I say something?" she asked. All eyes were on her. "You have been talking mostly about the corruption of the physical environment. However, I think this is, in itself, symptomatic of a moral corruption, which, I believe, goes to the core of the problem. It starts with the children."

Harry Elkin broke in with a passionate expletive, "Damn right it does! They cheat, they lie, and they steal. They do it right in the classrooms, but worst of all they intimidate the teachers."

"When I went to school the teachers intimidated us," Norman's wife Joan spoke up. "What do you mean, the children intimidate the teachers?"

"Well, I'll give you an example. You know my brother, Morry, the one who has the gift store in Niagara Falls. He and his wife, Frances, are both teachers. All the teachers have to take turns monitoring the halls. One day, Morry found two boys, both fifteen, smoking pot in the corridor, and he ordered them to put out their cigarettes. Instead, they both puffed in his face, and one of them told him to fuck off if he didn't want to have both his legs broken. I asked him what he did about it."

"'Did about it?' Morry said. 'What could I do? I would like to have beaten the crap out of them. Instead I reported them to the principal's office, and asked that these hoodlums be expelled. Do you know what happened? The parents complained that I was harassing their boys, and I, not them, was given the warning.'"

"What happened?" Joan asked.

"He took early retirement. Now he's getting a pension, and we are paying for it. And he's able to spend more time in the gift store."

"Was his wife harassed too?"

"No. She's still teaching."

"Come on now," said Lennie Greenberg, who had not uttered a word all evening. "The kids you describe are an isolated case."

Everybody was joining the debate. Margie, Harry's wife, reacted, "Isolated case, indeed! They are growing in numbers every day. Morry's harassment occurred in Niagara Falls. But there was an incident right here, in Toronto, at one of the local high schools, where half a dozen high school boys ganged up on a female teacher. You must have read about it in the papers. These delinquents had formed a neo Nazi club. The teacher was Jewish, and when she entered the room they stood up in unison and gave the Nazi salute, shouting, 'sieg heil.'"

"What paper was it in?"

"Both the *Tely* and the *Star*. And I believe it was also on the radio."

"What school was it at?"

"I believe it was at Tech. The teacher was moved to another school."

There was a lull as the implication of the incident began to sink in. Calman then continued:

"You see, I agree that there are exceptions. But the numbers are growing, and the incidents are also becoming more violent. Are the kids at fault? Today, a teacher cannot discipline these rowdies, and if, God forbid, he does, the school can be sued and he can be fired. And there's another thing…these troublemakers are not just confined to boys. The number of girl rowdies is also increasing."

David Garfinkle took out a cigar, and was about to light up, when one of the women pinched her nose between her thumb and forefinger, signaling her disgust, "Ugh! He's going to stink up the room."

"David is that one of those smelly stogies?" the perky red-haired hostess, Joan Walters piled on.

"They're not smelly," Lennie, laughed, "They're genuine nickel cigars."

"Well," said David in excuse. "The conversation was getting heavy, and I can think better when I smoke. But…" and he stood up and bowed to Joan. "Out of respect to mine hostess, I will refrain from smoking. Has anybody got any tobacco I can chaw on?"

He returned to his seat, and directing his attention to Calman. "So Cal, you blame the government for the problems of the world. What about the poor assholes who elect them?"

His wife, Alice, stopped him, "You know, David, I don't like you to use that kind of language."

"What! You don't like the word 'asshole'? It's a very fitting description, don't you think? Let's take a vote."

"Shut up David," said someone else. "Make your point."

"My point is that blaming the government for failures is a cop out. I believe in the individual. Every person is responsible for himself. If too many individuals act without thinking during election time, they have no one but themselves to blame."

Someone said, "Power corrupts, and absolute power corrupts absolutely."

"Who coined that phrase?" Norman asked.

"I recall that Dalton Camp used it in an article after his big blow-up with Diefenbaker, though I'm not sure that he actually originated the phrase," Calman remarked.

Dr. Caplan, now added, "I've heard that expression before. I think there was an eighteenth century English writer by the name of Cary…Henry I believe, who translated a number of the classics. I think it was a quote from Pindar."

Calman picked up the thread of the conversation again, "Norman, now the party's getting esoteric. Let's sponsor him for Trivial Pursuits."

A murmur passed through the group, and Calman continued, "There are all kinds of indicators out there pointing in the direction the world is taking."

"And what road is that, Cal?"

"The road to hell…to moral decay."

"Be specific please."

"What about the promiscuity amongst youth, for example. I don't want to sound Victorian, but I think it's gone too far when it is being flaunted in our faces, every day. It is becoming embarrassing for a girl to admit she's a virgin. Did you know that there's an inexpensive pill on the market, which a woman can take to prevent pregnancy? Of course you do! So now they can fuck all they want without the fear of consequences. And those who don't indulge are becoming the outcasts. And this is being abetted by the powerful pharmaceutical lobby."

"What other signs are there of this moral decay, Cal?" The question came from David, and Calman felt that he was being baited. But he took up the challenge.

"Divorce! Did you know that, in the United States, one out of every four marriages ends in divorce? And studies indicate that this trend will continue to increase. How long do you think it will take before the same happens here? A phenomenon that is becoming common is 'open marriage', where a married couple lives together, have their meals together, raise their children in common, but each carries on his or her own sex life with whomever he or she pleases."

"Then there is this feminist movement…this woman Betty Friedan…"

"Hold it right there, Calman Mencher," Thelma piped in, "Are you about to tell us that a woman's place is in the home?"

"Did I say that, or even imply that? No, I don't believe that for a second. But I do find a kind of militancy amongst feminists, a sort of aggression, and I don't like it."

"Why should militancy, as you call it, be confined to men? Why not women? This notion that only men can wield authority is a myth, and this is the 'brave new world'. You had better get used to it gentlemen."

"Yes, Sir!" said David, and he stood up at attention, and saluted Thelma. "I wonder how many guys would like to sleep with a macho female." Thelma gave him a withering look, and he sat down chastised.

"O.K. Cal. What else!" Lennie interrupted. "Lay it all out on the table for us. What are the other signs of our corrupted morality?"

"All right, my friend: What about the gun laws? Any nut can go into a gun store and buy a revolver. You've all read the papers last week about the guy who walked into court carrying a gun, and killed the lawyer acting for his wife in their divorce case. He'll probably get ten years, with time off for good behaviour."

The conversation now swung back to political corruption. But it was getting late and the evening ended with a joke.

"A flamboyant politician walked into a restaurant and noticed a well-known comedian seated at a table having his meal. He walked over to the comedian, slapped him on the back, and said, 'Say there, aren't you the famous comedian, Hector Heckerman? Why don't you tell us a Joke?' The comedian turned around, stared angrily at his tormentor, and said, 'Aren't you the famous politician, Dickhead Fouler? Why don't you tell us a lie?'"

CHAPTER XXIV

The family was seated around the rectangular table – the three boys and three girls. Paul, the oldest, was in his first year of law, at Osgood Hall. He had invited his friend, Mike Harris, who shared quarters with him, to join the family for dinner. So, in fact, there were six young people. Carole was busy at the stove, and happy to have all her children together for a meal. Kenneth had been on the phone in the den, and he now walked into the dining room, and took his seat at the head. He was in a good mood.

"What's for dinner tonight?"

Eyes were averted from him, and no one answered. He looked at the youngest, "What's for dinner Maggie?"

"Roast," she answered timidly.

"Roast, eh! I hope it's not poisoned. Ha, Ha, Ha," he laughed. The youngsters squirmed. Sensing the discomfort he was creating, he turned his attention to their guest.

"How are you, Mike?"

"Fine, thank you, Sir," Mike replied.

"What have you and Paul been learning at law school?"

"Today's lecture was on torts."

"What the hell is torts?"

Paul stepped in, "In the broadest sense, Dad, it means a sort of civil wrong."

"Yeah! How can a wrong be civil?"

Carole placed a large platter on the table. The younger people waited for Ken to dig in. He loaded his own plate, and without another word, began to eat with a voracious appetite. Carole sat down at the opposite end of the table, next to Maggie.

Maggie nudged her, "Mom, could you help me with my homework this evening?"

"Why, of course dear. Now eat your dinner."

"Why can't you do your own homework?" Ken took the child to task. "Your mother and I are going out tonight."

The child started to whimper, and Carole patted her head, "Don't worry dear; I'll help you with your homework."

"Are you deaf?" Ken berated his wife. "I said we're going out tonight." He rose from the table and strutted out. "Get dressed," he growled at her. "We're going to Bart Palmer's."

She felt abashed, and without a word, left the room, but in a few minutes returned to the young group. She beckoned the oldest girl, Lynne, who was drying the dishes. "Lynne, I have to go somewhere with Dad. Will you help Maggie with her homework?"

"Of course, Mom!" And she took her mother's arm. "Look Mom, you don't have to go with him." The emphasis on 'him' as the others formed a protective circle around Carole, which gave her a feeling of safety from Ken. At the same time, she was disconcerted, and did not want them to witness her quarrel with her husband.

Carole went into the bedroom and changed into a navy skirt and jacket, which made her look prim, and smart. She did not like Bart. He was one of the vulgarians with whom Ken associated. She had not met Bart's wife, nor had she met the wives of any other of Ken's band of friends, and knew she would feel uncomfortable in their company, sort of out of sync.

Ken rang the bell, and a smiling, somewhat tipsy Bart opened the door, waving a glass of rum.

"Well," he chortled: "The ole fart finally got here."

Ken was now in good humour, "Hey! Be careful the way you swing that glass; you may lose a few drops." Carole felt awkward, and became irritated by their banter.

They followed Bart into the house. Lillian, a tall, stringy, dyed blonde, came to introduce herself. "Hello, I'm Lillian, Bart's wife. You must be the doctor, Ken's wife."

She extended her hand to Carole. Carole shook her hand, "My name is Carole."

Ken spoke up, "Hey, Bart, where's the entertainment?"

"There's a poker game in the other room. The drinks are on the table over there." He pointed to a table laden with different bottles of liquor.

"Help yourself." Lillian handed Carole a bottle of beer. No glass.

Carole found a chair, tucked into a little alcove. She sat down, and tucked her legs in, and then placed the unopened beer bottle on the floor. Two women approached her and one introduced herself.

"I'm Geraldine Smythe. My husband is Tex, the drunken oaf standing over there, talking to your husband, and this is Mary Jackson."

The two women pulled up some chairs, and placed them in front of Carole, and sat down. Each downed her drink. Carole could smell the liquor on their breath, and was revolted by the stench. A few more of the ladies came over to meet The Doctor. Carole was plied with questions about her work, and her family, and background.

She was uncomfortable with these people, and, excusing herself, went to look for Ken. She found him in another room with the guys. He was smoking a cigar, drinking whisky and gambling. She realized that this was his milieu. Nothing she could do would change him. She left the room, found a phone in the kitchen, and phoned for a cab, leaving Kenneth to indulge in his favorite pastime.

On the drive home in the cab, Carole contemplated her fate.

How could I have been so blind? I should have foreseen the direction my life was taking. The best part of my life is the children. Tomorrow I will have it out with Ken. I'll give him an ultimatum. I don't want his friends in our house anymore. He's to make up with the Airline Company who fired him, and try to get his job back. Yes, and he's to stop bullying the kids and me. Also, there's to be no more drinking.

That evening, she moved her clothes out of the bedroom into her office, and locked the door.

CHAPTER XXV

Calman had moved his offices to the Yonge/Sheppard, in the north-central part of Toronto, in 1962. A few days after Calman was installed in his new offices, Robert Carver dropped in to see him. Robert was a man about Calman's age who was a perennial optimist. He brought coffee and doughnuts, and they hit it off at once. Robert occupied the ground floor of the building, and Calman the floor above, and he became Calman's newest client. Rob designed office furniture, and Calman was surprised to discover how large the demand was for his design services.

"What kind of furniture do you design?" Calman asked.

"Chairs," came the unexpected reply.

"Only chairs?" Calman asked in surprise.

"I have also designed some filing systems. But basically I design chairs."

"This is incredible. How can you be kept busy just designing chairs?"

"Well the fact is that I'm very busy right now designing for several clients."

"What kind of fees do you charge?"

"Only nominal."

"I don't understand. How do you survive? And you also design filing systems. In what way do your files differ from the regular pull-out files?"

"They're radial."

"What do you mean?"

"Come downstairs, and I'll show you. They are circular."

"Circular! Hmmm. It seems to me that I read an article a few months ago about circular filing cabinets. Where was that? It could have been in *Time* magazine."

"That was me."

"Was that your picture on the cover of *Time*?"

"That was me."

Robert had grown up in the Canadian east coast, and at an early age, he developed a love of sailing and fishing. During World War II, he had enlisted in the Navy, and by the end of the war, had become a seasoned sailor. His secretary referred to him, affectionately, as 'The Admiral'. One summer day Robert walked up to the second floor into Calman's office.

"Is Cal in?" he asked the receptionist.

"Oh, hello Mr. Carver," she said. "I'll let him know you're here." She dialled Calman, and he came right out.

"Hello Rob. What's up?"

"Can you break away from your heavy schedule this afternoon? I want to show you something."

"Who am I seeing this afternoon," Calman asked his secretary.

"Mr. Lindsey."

"Oh, him! He's been trying to sell me furniture for two months." He turned to his secretary: "Tell him to leave the brochures, and I'll call

The Chaplin Cane

back tomorrow." He then turned back to Robert: "How long will this take, Rob?"

"The rest of the day."

Turning back to the receptionist, he said, "I guess I won't be back today. If Mrs. Mencher calls, tell her I might be late for dinner."

He started to walk toward the stairway after Carver, "OK. Rob, where are we going?"

"We're off to the Port Credit Yacht Club. That's where my boat is docked."

"What boat?"

"My new CC16," Rob announced proudly. "We're going to take her for a sail." Calman had never sailed before, and he had a few questions.

"Does this mean that the length of the boat is sixteen feet?"

"Yes, with an eight foot beam. That is the width. I can see you don't know much about sailboats. But you're going to love it. I'll teach you how to sail, and soon you'll have your own boat."

Robert parked the car, and they walked over to the dock. Calman was given a short three-minute sailing lesson, and Robert maneuvered the boat into the middle of Lake Ontario. As the boat came about, Robert hollered 'hard to lee', and Calman did not require a lesson to know what to do. He ducked, and barely avoided going overboard into the lake.

Calman spent the day at the helm learning how to lean into the wind, to trim the sails taut, and to allow them to luff and shake. Robert was at the sails, hoisting, heaving and unfurling

"Does this boat have a name?" Calman asked.

"Yes, *The Ariel*."

"*The Ariel*?" Calman repeated. Did you know that the poet, Percy Bysshe Shelley sailed a boat called *The Ariel*?"

"How did you know that?" Robert was surprised. That's how I got the name."

"Shelley is my favorite poet, and has been so since the days of my youth."

"You surprise me, Cal. I've never known an accountant with poetic inclinations. Most of them are plain-speaking, unromantic, and practical-minded businessmen."

"Well there you are; another myth exploded." A bond was now established between the two men, and after this day they sailed together every Friday afternoon during the summer months.

It was on one of these sailing expeditions that Robert told Calman that he had been awarded the contract to build the Maritimes Pavilion for the forthcoming World's Fair to be held in Montreal in 1967.

"Congratulations," Calman said warmly. "But it seems to me that you don't have very much time. You have barely a year. Are you sure you will be able to meet the deadline?"

"No problem. I speculated on winning the contract. So I went ahead on my own and completed all the drawings."

"Including the specs?"

"Everything. I've even engaged a general contractor."

"What kind of design do you have in mind?" Calman asked.

"The building will be shaped like a boat."

"I might have guessed," Calman laughed. "It's a clever idea, and very appropriate for the Maritimes."

There was a silence between them, so Calman continued, "Rob, as you know, I'm very glad for you. But you should never second-guess your chances of getting a contract. What would you have done if your bid had not been accepted?"

Rob said nothing, and as the winds were shifting and the waters getting rough, they turned the boat and headed for shore.

During the construction phase of the Montreal World Fair, Rob had to make frequent trips to the site. On one of these trips, he met a man by the name of Trinka, a Czech artist who had created life-sized doll puppets. These puppets, Calman was to reflect on later, might well have been the forerunner of the Muppets. The affable Robert established a close rapport with this Trinka.

Shortly after the World Fair opened, Calman drove his family to Montreal, and through his many connections in the city was able to obtain a hotel room at Ruby Foo's. Once settled into the hotel they were off to the Fair. The site was vast, a fairyland of musicians, dancers, clowns, of goblins, elves and sprites.

"Is this the land of Oz?" Elizabeth asked.

"No dear," Ruth replied, "It's just a place to have fun and to see all kinds of exhibits, and learn about other parts of the world. Make notes so that you can tell your teacher about all the things you saw."

The buildings were of every size and shape, with varicoloured roofs, gables, spires and pinnacles. There were large line-ups of people waiting to get into the different pavilions, and hundreds of people milling about speaking every language…English, French and Russian, Hungarian, Spanish, Italian, Chinese.

Ruth nudged Calman, "This is a sort of microcosm of the world, except that, here, everybody is always happy, and there are no wars."

"Yes." Calman re-joined, "This is a temporary Utopia, a dream world where everybody gets along. Then comes the rude awakening into the real harsh world. Let's enjoy the afternoon."

Elizabeth tugged at her father's coat sleeve, "Daddy, look at that big boat."

"Well, I'll be darned!" Calman exclaimed, "That must be the Maritimes Pavilion, you know, the one that Robert built. Let's go through it."

About a month after the Fair had closed, Robert phoned Calman, and asked him to join him for lunch at the Friars Club in downtown Toronto. When Calman arrived, Robert was already seated at a table with two other gentlemen. As Robert started the introductions, the others started to rise, but Calman motioned to them to remain seated.

"This is Calman Mencher, my accountant," Robert explained. "Cal, this is Douglas Horner. They shook hands, "and Daniel Morrison."

"Would you care for a drink?" Horner asked."

"What are you gentlemen drinking?"

"Wine!" Robert beckoned to the waiter."

"Cabernet Sauvignon!" Calman said with authority. He then turned to Horner:

"What do you do Douglas?"

"Please call me Doug."

"O.K. Call me Cal."

"I'm an architect."

Robert spoke up, "Doug is very creative. He designed the Planetarium in Halifax a few years ago, and recently he designed, and built, the Toronto Planetarium. It's located next to the museum on University Avenue. Have you seen it?"

"Yes I have," Calman replied. "My wife and I went down about two weeks ago. It was quite an experience. One has the sensation of being in outer space. It was most impressive. Congratulations, Doug."

Robert interjected again. "Cal is himself interested in astronomy. Isn't that right, Cal?"

"That's a hobby I'm giving up. I hate working on logarithmic problems, which is ninety percent of the science. And what is your field?" Calman faced Daniel.

"I'm a psychiatrist."

"I get it!" Calman said cheerfully. "There was a furniture designer, a planetarium builder, an architect and an accountant who met at the Fryer's."

However no one was paying attention to Calman's attempt at humour. All eyes were riveted on the far end of the large room. He beheld several young women, nude to the waist, baring their amply endowed breasts. Male patrons were taking turns painting their navels, and their breasts. One of the patrons was painting red and blue circles around the nipples of one of the girls, who giggled at him.

"I don't care for the main course, but I like the looks of the dessert menu," Doug quipped.

"My office is just around the corner," said Daniel dryly. "Let's take a walk over there, and we can continue our talk in privacy. I'll order some sandwiches to be sent up."

They rose in unison to leave, and Robert started singing the theme song from the Bob Hope T.V. show, playing on the word 'memories' – "Thanks for the mammaries."

The four men sat in a circle around the coffee table in Daniel's office. Calman looked at his watch.

"Will someone please explain to me why we are gathered here?"

"We want to form a company," said Robert. "The purpose will be to write, and produce, educational films for children. We are inviting you to join us."

Calman did not try to disguise his surprise.

"Why would you want me to be a part of this enterprise?"

"I've already filled in Doug and Dan on your background, especially your interest in literature," Robert explained.

"But," Daniel added, "Quite frankly, Cal, the input we really want from you is business and organization. We need to raise money for the project, and Robert thought you could be of help in this area."

Both Robert and Douglas turned crimson at Daniel's plain talk.

Boy! This guy doesn't mince words, Calman thought.

"Have you completed any scripts yet?" Calman enquired.

"Yes! Seven, and another twelve in process," Robert answered quickly.

"Do you have any copies here of the completed ones?" Cal asked. Robert probed into his briefcase and withdrew several sheaves of paper, and handed them to Calman. "Would you mind if I take these home? I would like to read them this evening. I'll return them to Robert tomorrow morning."

"You are aware, of course, that they're copyrighted," Daniel said. Calman made a decision right then. He did not like this man. But he carried on, not wishing to offend Robert. The meeting lasted for another half hour, and then adjourned. Robert was voted in as president of the company, which had no existence as yet, and Dan and Doug each became vice-presidents. When they proposed Calman as secretary-treasurer, he politely declined.

"I haven't decided yet whether I want to take a position in your company."

Later that evening, after dinner, Calman put on his slippers, sat down at his desk, and filled his pipe. Ruth brought him a heated snifter of brandy; comfortably ensconced in his large leather chair, he started to read the scripts. None of the scripts exceeded twenty pages. After reading the first script, he handed it to Ruth. He had already given her an account of his meeting at the Fryer's and later at Dr. Morrison's.

"Read these, Ruth, and tell me what you think of them." She sat down on the large cushioned sofa, crossed her legs, and started to read. After some twelve minutes, she put down the sheaves of paper.

"These plays are very short," she observed.

"Yes, that's the idea. They're being written for television…half hour slots…fifteen minutes of film, and fifteen minutes of advertising," he explained. "Morrison, the psychiatrist of the group, thinks that they have to be brief, very brief, to hold the attention of the children."

"Well," said Ruth. "I think the content is good. But it's too short. It should be at least a half hour."

"I think he's right. They're brief, exciting and funny. Plenty of slapstick! They also have to possess educational content, which I think they have."

"So why do they want you to read these scripts?"

"That's what I've been wondering. I believe that Robert really appreciates my opinion. Doug Horner, who is somewhat of a quiet intellectual, also, I think, values my input. But this fellow, Daniel…"

"The psychiatrist?"

"Yes, doesn't give a damn as to what I think. He has the idea that I'm loaded, and he wants me to fund the project. But he won't put up five cents of his own money."

"What about the others?"

"Robert, I know for a fact, hasn't got a spare nickel, and Douglas, I'm sure, barely ekes out a living. Morrison has made it clear that he wants to be paid on a regular basis. So who needs him as a partner?"

On the following day, Calman telephoned Robert, and told him that he could not serve as secretary for his company.

"I read all seven of your completed scripts, and I see potential in them. But neither of your friends has a clue about business, and Dr. Morrison is going to cause trouble for you."

"Cal, are you in your office now?"

"Yes, why?"

"I want to show you something. I'll be right there."

Robert skipped by the receptionist, and charged right into Calman's office. Calman was impatient.

"Look here Rob, I can't spend any more time on this scheme of yours. I have other clients to see."

"I understand Cal, and if you don't want to participate with us, then bill me for the time you've spent."

Calman looked at him sheepishly as he opened the folder and withdrew two letters.

"I have an appointment next week with two potential customers. Both of them want to bid for the exclusive rights. Both will finance the entire project. I want you to come with me to New York."

"Who are these potential patrons?"

"They are Columbia Pictures, and the Encyclopaedia Britannica."

"Let me see the letters."

Robert handed him the letters, and Calman began to read.

"All it says here is that they are interested in new products."

"Don't you see? That is as good as a contract?"

"Well you better call to make sure they'll see us."

Robert already had the plane tickets, and within a few days, they flew to New York. Their first visit was to Columbia. They climbed up two flights of stairs, and Robert went directly up to the receptionist, and asked to see the company president. She asked him if he had an appointment.

"Yes," he answered and handed her his card. She spoke into the intercom and after a few moments looked up at Robert.

"I'm sorry, sir, but Mr. Henderson is not in the office. His secretary has no record of an appointment with you. Are you sure you're in the right place?"

The Chaplin Cane

Calman, observing what was happening, was embarrassed and chagrined. This, he remembered, was typical of Robert. On the slightest hint of encouragement, he would conclude he had a deal, and would proceed to prepare designs, which he would present to the astonished prospective client. The receptionist realized his mistake, and felt sorry for them.

"Just a minute," she said. "I'll see if someone else can see you." After a twenty-minute wait they were ushered into an underling's small office. Robert immediately started in on his pitch, but the interviewer, who, it seemed to Calman, was a freshman just out of school, raised his hand to stop him.

"I'm very sorry gentlemen, but I think you're in the wrong place. We don't handle educational shorts. The concept is very interesting, but you should be talking to some of the T.V. stations, or a school board."

Once in the street Robert began to rationalize. "Did you hear what he said…the concept is very *interesting.*"

Calman did not bother to respond.

They arrived at the building that housed the *Encyclopaedia Britannica*, and, this time, Robert did have an appointment. Mr. James Emory came out to greet them. His office was larger, and more luxurious than the last office they had visited.

"Gentlemen," he greeted them, "May I offer you a coffee?"

"Thank you," they both accepted. Robert was again in an exuberant mode.

Here he goes, again," Calman thought. *He'll interpret the coffee offer as a deal, signed and sealed.*

The coffee was brought in and Mr. Emory started, "I have read your scripts and I like them, but there are only seven. How many more have you completed?"

Robert didn't hesitate.

"Twenty-two, and we can have another twenty by the end of the month."

"We would want to be certain that you have at least one hundred scripts before shooting commences. How long would it take you to do that?"

"Two to three months," Robert assured him.

"You realize that precision is very important. Each showing will have to run for exactly two minutes. But we can deal with this problem during the editing."

Calman nodded, and motioned to Robert not to interrupt. "Now, have you decided yet on what medium to use?"

Robert thought for a minute. "We have given some thought to it, but have not yet reached a decision. We can let you know before the end of the week."

"Do you have a card?

They exchanged cards.

"Here is our proposal. You will do the writing and the production. We only want to see the finished product. We will pay all hard production costs. We will not pay for the writing, or any travelling, or incidental expenses. Nor will we pay for any prototype, and we want to see three prototypes before we commit to anything."

Calman was fearful that Robert was going to let out a whoop, but instead he merely exclaimed, "It looks like we have a deal!"

Robert was clearly in high spirits.

"Just a minute," Calman interposed. "We haven't yet heard the terms."

"I'm coming to that," Emory said. "We will pay you five thousand dollars for each script that we accept, from which we will deduct the hard production costs already paid for by us. The scripts will belong to us to deal with as we please. In addition to the five thousand, you will be entitled to a royalty of two per cent on all income we earn from your scripts.

Calman spoke up again: "Is that gross income?"

"Yes, of course!"

Calman intervened again. "I would like to make a counter proposal. We will guarantee a minimum of one hundred and twenty scripts per year, and you will pay us the greater of five thousand dollars per script, or five hundred thousand dollars per annum. This allows you to reject twenty scripts."

"No," Emory replied, "But we will agree that if you do not make five hundred thousand dollars annually from us that you will be free to terminate the contract." Emory looked at his watch. "I will send you a letter of intent in a couple of days."

Robert and Calman left to catch the flight home.

After flying back to Toronto, Robert gathered around his partners.

"We will have to use live model," said Daniel.

"That could be very expensive," Calman replied.

"Who cares? They're paying."

"No they're not. They're paying five thousand dollars per script, and if it becomes uneconomical for them, they'll cancel."

"Why can't we use cartoons?" Doug asked.

"Because live models are better," said an exasperated Daniel.

"What about puppets?" Robert joined in. "I met this Czech fellow in Montreal during the World Fair. His puppets were the talk of the Fair. They are large, almost human size. I'm going to try to contact him."

"I've heard of him," said Doug. "I hear he's incredible."

"If we don't use live models count me out," Dan insisted.

"Let's take a vote," Cal chimed in. "All in favour of live models?"

Dan raised his arm. "O.K. All in favour of caricatures? No one? O.K. All in favour of puppets?" Rob, Doug and Calman raised their arms.

"Carried," said Cal. Dan rose, put on his hat and coat, and walked out. He paused at the door and announced, "I'll send you my bill."

On the following day, Calman telephoned Robert to determine whether the group could carry on without Daniel, But Robert's secretary, Linda, informed him that Robert was out of town. "He had left for Prague."

When Robert returned a few days later, he phoned Calman.

"Well," he said ruefully, "We'll not be dealing with Trinka. He died a few days before I arrived. I visited his widow before returning. Cancer! All of his creative work is now bogged down in his estate. It will take years to unravel."

Daniel sent Robert a bill for his time, and Robert sent Daniel a much larger bill for his time, and for Daniel's portion of the costs to travel to New York and Europe.

The experiment in educational films was not an entire loss to Calman. Six months after the break-up of the group of 'four wise men,' he received a call from Dr. Daniel Morrison.

"Hello, Cal," he said, "I've been invited to moderate a discussion between Marshall McLuhan and Northrop Frye, and I'm permitted to have a few friends attend. Would you and your wife care to join us?" Calman was overwhelmed.

"We would be honoured."

CHAPTER XXVI

Twenty full years had gone by since Calman had spoken to Dr. Carole Williston. He had put on a few pounds, and had grown balder. Ruth's girlish waist had expanded a little, but she still possessed a luxurious hourglass figure, and was a splendid, elegant woman…wise and witty. She now conducted her marriage-counselling practice from their home, which hummed with the comings and goings of strangers, family, and friends seeking her advice.

Elizabeth, who had been given the pet name of Bep, was now nineteen, and was a student of drama at a Boston University. Their son, Barnett, was seventeen, and completing high school. Calman's accounting practice had flourished, and he now had several partners. Their offices were situated at Bloor and Yonge Streets, one of Toronto's most prestigious locations.

The intercom buzzer sounded.

"There's a lady on the phone for you, but she won't give me her name, and I don't recognize her voice," said Audrey, the receptionist.

"OK.", he said, "put her through." He had not thought about Carole in all these years, but when the soft, hesitant voice said, "Hello Calman." he responded instinctively.

"Why, hello Carole, How are YOU?"

"I'm just fine. I was concerned you would not remember me after all this time." There was a pause, as if she needed assurance to continue. "I hope you are not angry with me." Amused, he recalled that these were the very words with which she had ended their last conversation.

He replied good-naturedly, "I was never angry with you, and you should banish such thoughts. So, is there anything I can do for you?"

"Well, yes," she said, "Our medical practice has broken up, and I am now practising on my own again. I was wondering if you would take me back, as a client.

"It would be a pleasure," he assured her. He looked at his calendar, and gave her an appointment at his office later in the week. It occurred to Calman, as he hung up the phone, that their past meetings had always been held on her terrain. Now she was coming to him, and despite himself, he felt a current of power surge through his body. He went to the kitchen, and brewed a cup of coffee. Settling back in his large leather chair, and enjoying the brew, he thought to himself, *the partnership has broken up. Hmmm! I wonder if anything else has broken up.*

The buzzer sounded. "Dr. Williston is here for her appointment," Audrey announced.

"Thank you. Have her take a seat. I'll be with her shortly." Calman quickly gathered up the papers that cluttered his desk, and deposited them in a drawer. He then dusted off the desktop, and placed a note-pad, and two sharpened pencils, on the desk. He wanted Carole to see a neat, and orderly desk, to convey an impression of efficiency. As he walked through the hallway towards the reception area, he checked his jacket to make sure there were no stains or bulges. Assuming an air of nonchalance, he entered the reception area where she was seated. Calman walked swiftly towards her, all smiles, and extended his hand in greeting.

His mind telescoped back twenty-five years, when she proffered her outstretched hand to him. She gave him a deferential nod, taking him in with the same smiling eyes. He noted that her facial lineaments were sharper, and that her hips had fanned out a little. But she still had that wholesome robust look.

Calman led her to his office, and observed her scanning the room…the oak desk, several framed diplomas on the wall, the Persian rug. He saw her taking in the Carmichael painting that hung on the wall behind and above his desk.

"Group of Seven?" she queried. Calman nodded. She was impressed. There was a short interval of awkward silence. She was now in Calman's domain. Here, he presided, and he commanded respect. He wanted her to see him in the role of busy practitioner with no time for chitchat. At the same time, though, he did not want to appear officious. She was vulnerable, and he was playing a game for which he was later ashamed.

"Well, shall we get down to business?" he said. She opened her briefcase, and produced a file containing her income tax returns and financial statements. Calman started to scan them and was surprised at the meagre income her practice was producing. He shook his head and looked up at her. Her eyes were misty.

"How much time did you put into the practice?"

"Three days a week."

"What about your partners? Did they also work three days per week?"

No, they worked a full week."

"And how was your share of the partnership income determined?"

"According to my billings."

"What about the firm's expenses? You know, medical supplies and so forth, rent, staff salaries. How were they shared?"

"Equally!"

"Equally? Are you certain? Was there a partners' agreement?"

"Yes!"

"And was this equal sharing of expenses pursuant to the agreement?"

"I'm not certain." She seemed confused. "But I think it was. You see, they contended that I was free to work five days a week if I wanted to."

"Were you the only oral surgeon in the firm?"

"Yes!"

"Did most of your referrals come from your partners?"

"Some. However, once I joined the partnership, my other referral sources began to dry up. In retrospect, I guess the partnership was not such a good move."

"Hmmm!"

"That is why I finally dropped out of the partnership," she said sadly. Calman made no reply, but continued to scan the returns.

"I don't see any investment income here." Haven't you been earning any?"

"I don't have any." He looked at her somewhat bewildered. "Well, you see," she said shakily, "Kenneth…"

"Kenneth?" Calman nearly choked, "Ken is now Kenneth. How formal."

"…Took over the management of my portfolio after I, ahh, we…" she was distressed; Calman was afraid she was going to cry. "…After you ceased advising me."

She handed Calman a list of stocks. There was not a blue chip among them. Speculations, all! He had been gambling with her money… oils, base metals, paper, timber, railways, silver. Gee, some were already off the board.

"Kenneth," he muttered to himself. "That stupid son-of-a-bitch." His mind must have been transparent because she blushed. There was a long silence during which this lovely, genteel, educated woman, who faced Calman Mencher, came to the full realization that she was insolvent. She started to fidget. Then she blurted out

"You know, I'm divorcing Ken."

It's damned well time, he thought. She had read his mind again, and felt impelled to explain. Kenneth had been born with a belligerent streak, she told him, but she had not recognized this during the first five years of their marriage. As time went by, his temper worsened. His worst abuses had started three years previously, when he ran afoul of his employers. He had refused to accept changes of flight schedules, and when he repeatedly failed to report as ordered, he was threatened with dismissal. He filed grievances and complained to the union, but they could do nothing for him. He then threatened to sue the union.

He was so obstinate that, eventually, he found himself persona non grata both in the union and the company. He was called down to the head office, dismissed, and handed a significant severance cheque, which he promptly tore up. He remained at home, sleeping late, unshaved, wandering about the house in his pajamas watching television, drinking and becoming increasingly sullen.

Calman had heard enough, and he brought the subject back to the business at hand. They agreed to meet once each year at Calman's office to discuss her finances. At tax time, one of the juniors in the office would prepare her financial statements and tax returns, and Calman would review them.

That evening, after dinner, Calman described the meeting with Dr. Williston to Ruth, who observed, "Well, things do have a way of coming around full circle."

CHAPTER XXVII

Shortly before Ruth and Calman were married, they had gone to their favourite French restaurant, La Maison D'oré, for dinner. As usual, Calman had ordered a snifter of Cognac, and Ruth was enjoying a glass of wine, a Beaujolais. Calman had helped her select the wine

"It comes from Burgundy, and should have a full-bodied flavour," he said, smiling. They clinked glasses. After a short while, Ruth broke the silence, "Cal, what have you been reading lately?"

"There's a new Jewish writer emerging on the scene, and I've just finished reading his first novel. His name is Bellow."

"Are you referring to Saul Bellow?"

"Yes! He wrote a short novel called *Dangling Man*. "Have you read it?"

"I've heard of it. But, no, I've not read it. Tell me about it."

"It's the story of a young man, Joseph, who is alienated and insecure. Kafka must have influenced Bellow because, like Kafka's hero, Joseph K, we never learn if he has a surname, and this sets the tone of uncertainty that pervades the novel. The timing of the novel is World War II, and the incidents and characters are revealed to us through Joseph's journal.

"The plot is something as follows: the U.S. Draft Board has notified the hero that he is going to be called for military duty. He resigns his job, expecting to be called up, and as the novel opens we find him lingering aimlessly, waiting for his call-up, which has been delayed due to bureaucratic bungling. He becomes increasingly morose, and belligerent. He lashes out at his wife, his brother, his ailing father-in-law, his landlord, a neighbour, even an old acquaintance. But at the end, he decides to wait no longer. He goes down to the draft office and enlists, and is accepted. Almost immediately, there is a change in his life. He feels alive again. He and his wife grow closer. He accepts his brother's invitation to come to his club; he is reconciled to his friends. He goes from a state of isolation and repression to one of involvement and self-respect."

Ruth absorbed all that Calman had said about the novel. "It seems that Bellow is an existentialist."

"Yes, I believe so. And so am I. In this modern world, one cannot wait for fate to lead us by the nose. We have to take the bull by the horns, and twist. There are so many choices to make; we cannot wait for things to happen. We have to make them happen. We have to make choices, and take our chances."

Calman remained an ardent existentialist for more than thirty years. In 1974 something happened that had caused him to change his mind. Ruth had gone to her doctor for her annual check-up. The mammogram was clear…negative. She returned home pleased. Two days later, however, her doctor called. He had detected something that had previously escaped his attention. Could she come in the next day for a biopsy? Just routine.

Calman accompanied his wife to the Toronto General hospital on the following morning, arriving just before 8 a.m. Ruth was admitted at once, and Calman was asked to wait in a room on the first floor. No one else shared the room, and by ten o'clock he started to fidget. He called the office and spoke to Audrey, the receptionist. No! There were no calls for him. He explained where he was, and informed her that he might be all day. "Cancel my meetings for the day," he told her, then he sat down on the sole chair in the room. After a few minutes, he began to pace the floor.

There was a bed in the room, and he sat down on the edge of the bed just for the change. Then he returned to the chair. By noon, he walked out of the room, along the corridor to the lobby, and over to the receptionist.

"I would like to know what is taking so long for my wife to have a simple biopsy. I brought here at eight this morning, and she was to be out by nine."

"What is her name sir?" the girl in the white smock asked.

"Ruth Mencher." She scanned a list of patients, and picked up the phone. After a few moments, but what seemed an interminable time to Calman, she returned the phone to its cradle and turned to Calman.

"Please be patient sir. It's been a very busy day. We're doing our best. She'll be down shortly."

"What floor is she on? I'd like to go up to be with her."

"I'm sorry! Only medical staff is allowed there." And she repeated, "She'll be down shortly."

Calman bought a newspaper, and returned to the room. He started to read, but was unable to absorb anything. At two o'clock, he again approached the receptionist, and tried to keep the alarm out of his voice.

"You told me two hours ago that my wife would be down shortly. I want to know: what's the delay?"

"What's her name, sir?"

"Ruth Mencher." Once again she lifted the receiver, and after a few moments, turned back to Calman:

"She's getting ready to come down. About fifteen minutes."

Calman walked to the cafeteria, keeping a watchful eye towards the room in case he should miss Ruth. He ordered a coffee, and walked swiftly back to the room, spilling some of the coffee. He sipped the coffee, slowly, staring vacantly into space, too frightened to think. His mind was in a vacuum.

Four o'clock! Calman got up, and strode to the reception desk. There was a different receptionist at the counter, and she was talking on the phone. He grabbed the phone out of her hand.

"Where is my wife?" he screamed. "Tell me now."

She nodded at a guard, and people nearby began staring. The guard pinioned Calman's arms as two more guards arrived. They dragged him away, one of the guards trying to calm him. "Now take it easy sir, just settle down." They half carried, half dragged, Calman to the other end of the hall, and sat him down in a chair. Calman was shaking with fear and rage.

The receptionist approached them accompanied by a man of about fifty. Calman was always sizing people up, and he noticed that the man was greying at the temples. He was wearing a full-length white jacket.

"It's all right guards," he said, "He'll be all right." He turned to Calman:

"Mr. Mencher?" Calman nodded.

"I am Dr. Rogers. Would you follow me please?" He led the way back to the room, which Calman had vacated a short while before. Calman was unsteady on his feet. They no sooner entered the room than Dr. Rogers shut the door and addressed Calman.

"Mr. Mencher, your wife is very ill."

The doctor spoke quietly, and very rapidly, wanting to get his task over with as quickly as possible. "I'm sorry to tell you that she has cancer. It is very serious. It's located in the breast, and we have had to perform a mastectomy."

Calman did not know what a mastectomy was, but he guessed. The doctor continued, "It has already spread through the lymph glands. She has a short time to live, perhaps two to three weeks."

He turned around, and left the room, and disappeared before Calman could recover his voice. Calman screamed inwardly. He screamed silently… a gut-wrenching scream. He had a floating sensation, and realized he was without gravity. He knew that he was on the floor, but could not rise. He could only squirm on his back…Kafka's bug.

"Help!" But there was no sound. "Help!" He did not recognize his own voice. The door was pushed open and an orderly entered. He was being helped to his feet. Someone had pushed him onto a chair, and his head was being pushed forward. A nurse came in.

"I found him on the floor," the orderly said. "He must have fainted."

"Mr. Mencher," the nurse was solicitous, "Please try to pull yourself together. They're bringing your wife down now."

There was a rattling of wheels on the marble floors outside the door, and an orderly pushed the wheeled-bed into the room. Ruth lay on the bed, seemingly lifeless. Her hair was wet, and it lay in strands covering her face. Her face was grey, her eyes were closed. Then she opened them, and saw him standing there, tears welling his eyes. She smiled at him, and held out her hand. He took it, and buried his face in it.

"It's all right Cal," she whispered. "Everything will work out."

The nurse put her hand on Cal's shoulder, and gently squeezed it.

"Sir, you have to move just for a moment. We have to raise your wife onto the bed." When they left the room, Calman turned back to his wife. But she was sound asleep.

CHAPTER XXVIII

Ruth had met Dr. Allan Sherman shortly after she had begun her private practice as a marriage counsellor. Dr. Sherman was a psychiatrist with whom she consulted about her caseload, especially when she detected abnormal behaviour in any of her clients. The two became close friends, and eventually he became her personal confidante and mentor. Somehow Calman was never jealous of their relationship, even when Ruth spoke of him glowingly.

One evening, as Calman was working in his den over a set of financial working papers, Ruth brought him a cup of tea. Calman accepted the tea gratefully, rubbed his eyes, and closed the file.

"Are you through with your homework?" she asked.

"Yes, I think I'll call it a night."

"Cal, you are working too hard. We never seem to find time to talk. You also never find time to play with the children, anymore. You're even tied up at the office on Saturdays."

"Well, I have to work hard. I'm a principal of the firm, and I carry a lot of responsibility."

"Why is it that other executives can find the time during the week to play golf and go out evenings?"

He replied a little irritated, "I can't answer for the other executives."

"No, Cal. That is not an answer. When a man drives himself as you do there's got to be a psychological reason for it."

"What! Are you my analyst now?"

"Don't be silly. I just want our lives to be a little fuller."

Calman was trying to be rational. "Look, I provide well for the family. We have a nice home, the children are well clothed, we each have a car, and we take holidays. What more do you want?"

"You're talking about quantity. I want quality."

Calman stood up and stretched. "Ruth I'm too tired to discuss this now. I'm going to bed."

Calman slept fitfully for about three hours. When he awoke, he looked at his bedside clock. It was nearly two a.m. He felt vaguely agitated, and looked over at Ruth. He thought he heard a quiet sob. He turned to her:

"What's the matter Ruth?"

"I can't sleep."

"Are you upset because of our conversation?"

"Yes! I am!"

"Is it because of what I said?"

"No. It's because of what you did not say."

"I don't understand."

"You always walk away from a conversation when you don't want to hear something about our personal lives. It is because you fear you may have to make some changes to your attitudes, and habits, which will take time away from balancing your precious books? As a result, nothing ever gets resolved."

"OK. Tell me what you want me to do."

"Cal, I can't give you a specific order of what you should do. You see, that it's all in your attitude…your mental outlook. You're not even conscious of it. You work very hard…long, long hours…sometimes late into the night. You must think this is commendable. But it is not, because it has a great cost, the sacrifice of your family. The children and I are outsiders."

"But isn't this what marriage is about, a sort of harmonious division of labour? The wife is responsible for the children…hearth and home. The husband pays for everything."

"Oh, Cal, you're so old fashioned, so out-of-date. Your long hours at the office have become a habit, one that you inherited from your parents. They were so insecure that work was the only ethic they valued. You need help to overcome this obsession."

With resignation Calman asked, "What kind of help?"

"I want you to see Allan Sherman."

"Allan Sherman? The psychiatrist?"

"Yes!"

"Well, why didn't you say so in the first place? Of course, I'll see him, O.K?"

"OK. When will you call him?"

"First thing tomorrow…I mean today."

"Is that a promise?"

"It's a promise. Now can we get some sleep?" She snuggled in his arms, and they slept until awakened by the alarm clock at seven a.m.

CHAPTER XXIX

Calman sat in the clean, Spartan, hospital room holding his wife's hand as she lay very still. He was overwhelmed with despair, and he sought some solace from the great poets. But all that came to mind were the words of Tennyson:

"Break, break, break

On thy cold gray stones, O sea!

And I would that my tongue could utter

The thoughts that arise in me."

And, as the feeling of helplessness and despair welled up in him, he thought of Eliot's sad words from *The Love Song of J. Alfred Prufrock:*

"Let us go then, you and I, when the evening is spread out against the sky like a patient etherized upon a table."

Calman knew he could not continue this way. If Ruth woke up, and saw his face, she would read his thoughts of death. There was a phone in the room. He dialled Allan Sherman's office. Allan answered the phone. It was nearly six o'clock and his secretary had already left for the day, and he was just locking up.

"Hello!" he said, "Dr. Sherman here."

"Dr. Sherman," came Calman's quavering voice. "This is Calman Mencher."

"Yes, Calman," came the alarmed rejoinder. "What's wrong?"

"Dr. Sherman, I'm in the hospital with Ruth," and the words he had been unable to utter now poured forth in a sobbing torrent. Allan was shaken.

"Cal," he said, "Stay with her. If she wakes up, hold her hand. Make sure you tell her how much you love her. I'm on my way."

When Allan arrived, half an hour later, he found her bolstering Calman, giving him assurances. Allan brought with him a dozen yellow roses, which he placed at the edge of Ruth's bed. Calman thought of the day, years ago, when he had proposed to Ruth with a dozen yellow roses. With Dr. Sherman present, Calman's spirits began to rise.

"I'll step out for a while and give you two cronies a chance to talk," he said, and he stepped out into the hall.

CHAPTER XXX

A few days later, Calman received a call from Dr. Sherman. "Cal, we're moving Ruth over to the Princess Margaret Hospital."

"I'm glad to hear that," Calman replied, "I hate Dr. Rogers. He's an insensitive, ill-mannered boor." A few days later Calman was introduced to Dr. John Sutherland at the Princess Margaret. He was, Calman estimated, about ten years younger than himself, a kind and thoughtful man.

Ruth was sitting up in her bed at the Princess Margaret, and Calman sat on a chair reading to her from an article he had found in the *Toronto Star* about her friend, Dennis Burton, the artist.

"Look what it says here. The Art Gallery of Ontario has purchased his *Three Graces*, a burlesque of the famous work by Rubens. Do you remember the work?"

"Yes, Cal, didn't we see it in Amsterdam, or was it Antwerp? Three luscious plump nudes, holding hands, and dancing in a circle. Does it say how Dennis burlesqued them?"

"He put girdles on them."

"Oh! It must be a howl. We'll have to go see it."

The door opened and Dr. Sutherland entered.

He beamed at Ruth. "Can I get in on the joke?" Ruth told him about the Dennis painting, and he smiled. Then he looked at Calman.

"I'm glad you're here Mr. Mencher, because there is something I want to discuss with both of you. There is a new drug with which we are experimenting. It is called 'chemotherapy'. We would like to try it on Mrs. Mencher. Even if you are not cured, we think it will prolong your life."

"For how long?" Calman asked.

"Perhaps a year, or two."

"Yes, let's try it," Calman cried excitedly.

"However," the doctor explained, "There are some side effects. You will probably lose your hair, though it will likely grow back after you have ended the treatments. The second side effect is that you will probably become quite nauseous after each treatment."

Ruth joked, "Just think, Cal, of how much we'll save on hairdressers."

A year passed, and then a second. They were learning to cope with the ever present shadow of death. But life was back to normal. Calman went to his office every day, but he did not stay late. Ruth did her counselling from the house by appointment. They both saw Allan Sherman once a week. The difference from the past was that they now treasured each day. They vacationed in Europe, in Israel and in the United States. One day when Calman returned from his office, he found Ruth all smiles.

"O.K. What is it?" he said. "You look like the cat that swallowed the canary. What did you buy?"

"I didn't buy anything. But I saw our dream house today. It's a large two-storey house set in a forest glen, on a large lot, offf a ravine. The master bedroom is on the first floor, but the upper floor has four bedrooms, three of which have bathrooms ensuite. On the lot, I counted twenty-six genus of trees. The lot is large enough to put up a pool and a tennis court."

Calman smiled. He knew that the mention of the pool, and the tennis court, was a ploy to persuade him.

"But I'm afraid it may be too expensive," she added.

"Let's go see it this evening."

Two days later they put in an offer. It was accepted, and a few months later, Ruth was installed as mistress of her new home.

CHAPTER XXXI

Dr. Williston called to say that she had been delayed, and would be half an hour late for their appointment. As Calman's schedule was tight, and it was getting close to the noon hour, he suggested that they complete their business over lunch. Calman escorted her to a little French restaurant across the street from his office, where they were shown to a table overlooking Bloor Street. They both ordered a French Chablis, and then got right down to business.

In the two years since she had switched her account back to Calman, she had disposed of her junk bonds and stock, and with the help of Calman's old friend, Charlie Tepper had built up a respectable mortgage portfolio yielding ten and twelve per cent returns. She was pleased, very pleased. At the end of the luncheon, as they were taking their coffee, Carole made a surprise announcement.

"Did you know that I am Jewish?"

"Yes, of course!" It was her turn to be surprised. "How did you know that?" she asked, curious. "Well," he drawled. "Let's say I just know."

"But how did you know?" she demanded like an excited child.

"Once," Calman reminded her, "when I paid you a visit at the Medical Arts Building -- that was before you were married -- you introduced me to your mother, Mrs. Waitzer. Waitzer is a Jewish name I believe, is it not?"

"Oh, yes! I remember," she said reflectively. "I suppose you know that Ken and the children are Anglican. We belong to Saint Michael's Anglican Church."

Calman looked at his watch, saw that the hour was getting on. "I have to be getting back to my office."

He paid the bill, and they started to leave. As they reached the door of the restaurant, she placed her hand on his arm.

"Cal, my family, including Ken, have no inkling of my Jewish background. And so, should you have any occasion to meet them, please do not make any reference to this conversation."

He nodded assent, and they shook hands and parted. Calman walked across the street to his office, wondering, *Why should she confide to me a secret to which even the closest members of her family are not privy?*

He felt uncomfortable, drawn in, like a conspirator.

CHAPTER XXXII

Another year and a half went by, and Ruth was living a full and active life, carrying a caseload of clients with marital problems, whom she saw in the home library. The library was lined with oak panels on which hung a few paintings, mostly landscapes in water colour. They hung wherever there were not any shelves lined with books. In addition to the desk chair, and an armchair, the room contained two comfortable leather chairs and a leather sofa. The windows were covered with silk, brocaded curtains, which matched the rug. The desk top was wiped clean except for an ink stand containing two pen holders and a plaque on which was inscribed the words, *To Cal with love, Ruth* and a single notebook. All in all, the room was comfortable and was conducive to reading, and conversation.

Ruth was also making an occasional appearance on television, taking painting classes, and attending conferences. Although she was in constant touch with her doctors, she and Calman were beginning to hope that the cancer had gone into remission.

It was getting close to the end of the year, and Ruth surprised Calman by suggesting that they have a New Year's party at their home.

"Are you certain that you can manage a party?"

"I'm pretty sure I can if you will agree to have it catered."

"That's fine with me. Who would you like to invite?"

"Let me see. We should prepare a list…The Newmans, the Lyons, the Walters, the Rhineholdts, the Carvers…"

"Who are the Carvers?"

"You know! Your client, Rob Carver and his wife, Joan. They've had us to their place several times, and we've never reciprocated."

Calman said emphatically, "No! The Carters will not fit in with the rest of our friends." Calman had not told Ruth about Robert.

A few weeks before Ruth had been diagnosed with cancer, Robert Carver paid a visit to his accountant, and friend, Calman Mencher. It was Calman's first meeting of the day, and he had sent down for coffee and muffins.

"Robert, I've been meaning to speak to you for some time."

"I know what you're going to say. Don't worry Cal, I'll pay your fee. How much am I in arrears?"

"Rob, you don't owe me anything. I've written off your account. Will you have a muffin?"

"Yes, thanks. You don't have to write it off. I'm just having a temporary setback."

"Rob, I'm not talking about a setback. The fact is that you're insolvent."

"No, I'm not, or, not for long. I've got some new contracts pending. Besides, I've been offered an assistant professorship teaching design at Sheridan College."

"That's wonderful. I think teaching is your natural forte. Now you won't need offices, anymore, or a secretary. You can cut out all of your expenses, and start to recoup some of your losses."

"No! I've decided to retain my office because I'll be getting some major contract.

"Rob, listen to me. I think you're kidding yourself. You get these contracts because you underbid on them, and then you can't deliver. That's why you're in so much financial difficulty. By the way, why are you buying so much insurance? It seems to me that you have more than enough."

"Oh, that! You know, it's only term insurance. So it's pretty cheap."

In the following months, Calman had been preoccupied with Ruth, and he did not have a chance to see Robert again, although Robert and Joan did send her books and flowers.

One day Calman received a phone call from Robert's son, Adam: "Mr. Mencher," the young man said, "My dad is gone."

Calman had a moment of panic.

"Gone? What do you mean?"

"Dad went out alone for a sail. There was a squall, and *The Ariel* could not stand up to it. His body was found washed up on the shore of Lake Ontario."

The stunned silence was interrupted by the sound of the boy's voice.

"Sir?"

"Yes, yes. I hear you," Calman said in a somber tone. "When is the funeral?"

"It will be tomorrow at ten a.m. There will be a service followed by a cremation."

"Is that what he wanted, to be cremated?"

A cremation! My God! Calman went into shock, and then it seemed to him that he was floating, dreaming. In his reverie he imagined Robert being consigned to the flames, which were greedily licking at him and devouring him. He wondered: *Will he have any pain as he is being consumed? Woe! Woe!* He lamented, as he recalled the fearful words from Dante's Inferno: "Abandon all hope ye who enter here."

Calman hung up the phone, and his thoughts went back to their first sail together. He thought of the poet, Shelley, who also died in his sailboat, *The Ariel*, during a squall. He wondered also whether Rob had died accidentally.

Well, Calman thought, *Rob's widow, Joan, must be devastated, but, at least, Robert has left her financially secure with all that insurance.*

CHAPTER XXXIII

One evening, as Ruth and Calman were dressing for the opera, Ruth told him that she had received a telephone call from Dr. Williston. His eyebrows rose in surprise.

"What did she want?" he asked angrily.

"She's very pleasant. We had an enjoyable chat, almost half an hour."

"Uhu!"

"Adjust your tie," Ruth teased. "It's on aslant." She reached up and straightened it. She was wearing a subtle perfume, and she allowed him to hold her closely for a moment. He knew they would be making love that night.

"Dr. Williston invited us to a social evening at her home this Saturday, and I accepted."

Later, Calman dozed peacefully throughout the performance of *The Marriage of Figaro*.

The house had not changed. But it was older, and somewhat neglected. Vines twirled up along the face of the building, curling into the crevices. Some of the brickwork needed pointing, and the stone pathway looked decrepit. Once inside, Calman noticed a stain on the ceiling where water had seeped in through the roof. Two rooms were under lock, in retirement from use.

But the house still had character, a kind of decayed elegance.

He saw the solitary cane, in its stock, and was tempted to pick it up and give it a twirl. Carole embraced Ruth, as though greeting an old sorority sister. They disappeared arm in arm in animated conversation, leaving Calman to find his own way. The other guests, all medical colleagues of Carole included three couples and one bachelor, Frank, who served as host. Carole must have sung the Menchers' praises to the other guests, because when they entered the room, all stood up in unison to greet them. Calman felt self-conscious by this show of respect; Ruth accepted it with her usual aplomb.

They were entertained in the bay room, the semicircular windows looking out onto the garden. In the centre of the room was a teak coffee table, with arms at the sides, which Frank unhinged, and lifted, creating a larger area. Carole rolled in a little cart containing petite pinafore sandwiches, pastries and fruit.

The room contained a fireplace, and Frank saw to it that the fire was kept aglow. The conversation was polite, and stimulating, but they studiously avoided politics, religion and medicine. Carole brought in a coffee and teapot, and a tray of French pastries. She poured a coffee for Calman, which she placed on the table before him, and then handed him a plate containing a napoleon. Calman's mind went back many years ago as he recalled the incident with Ken. Calman wondered if Carole had the same thing on her mind.

At the end of the evening, there were warm embraces and handshakes. "We must do this again soon," said one of the ladies sincerely. On the way home Ruth commented effusively, "Why she's darling! You didn't tell me she was so charming. Let's invite her to dinner."

They went home and made love.

CHAPTER XXXIV

During Carole's soiree, Ruth had learned that her middle daughter, Joan, was studying drama at a college in New Brunswick, and that she was expected to come home for the Easter holidays. Bep was, likewise, a drama major at New York University, and she was planning to come for the Passover holidays. Ruth called Carole, and invited her to dine with the Mencher family one evening during the holidays. Carole was delighted.

The dinner started with a pate appetizer, and was followed by a broth with matzo balls (dumplings). The entrée consisted of a brisket of roast beef served with golden brown potatoes. Dessert was a lemon meringue pie, which Ruth had baked herself.

The two girls hit it off at once, and the conversation was abuzz with theatre talk and anecdotes.

After dinner, the girls withdrew to Bep's room, from which came a steady flow of tittering and laughter. Ruth and Carole cleared the table, carrying on their own banter, while Calman walked the golden Labrador, Max.

Driving home that evening, Carole was quiet and pensive behind the steering wheel. Joan was also reflective.

"What is so absorbing?" Carole asked her daughter.

"I wish that Bep was my sister," the young woman replied.

"But you've got four siblings already."

"Yes. They're okay but she's special."

"Who knows, let's not wish it, but it may come to pass."

CHAPTER XXXV

Carole got off the elevator, and came hurrying down the corridor. She entered Calman's offices breathless. "I hope I'm not too late," she gasped to the receptionist.

"No, you're just on time. Take a seat Doctor and I'll let Mr. Mencher know you're here." She called Calman on the intercom, and turning again to Carole, said, "He'll be right out."

Calman appeared all smiles, and Carole stood up to greet him. They shook hands. He led the way to his office, and she breezed in behind him carrying her purse, and a briefcase. He went to his desk and motioned her to take a seat. He sat facing her.

"How is Ruth?" she asked.

"Fine," he said, opening a file that lay on his desk, and extracting some papers.

"Will Bep be coming home for the summer holidays?"

"I don't think so. She has a summer job in New York."

He now held a report in his hands and without glancing up, remarked, "Well, well! The income from your practice is really growing. Not only are your billings going up, but your expenses are coming down."

He fingered another report. "Aha! Are you aware that the income being generated from your investment portfolio is almost as much as your practice?"

"Are you pleased?"

She smiled. "Oh, yes. I'm very happy Calman."

"Well," he said, "We're going to have to increase your quarterly income tax instalments. Do you have any questions?"

"Yes. I have been thinking of modernizing my office facilities and buying some new equipment."

"Well, first, is it necessary, and, second, what will it cost?"

"I think I could defer it for a year, but it will have to be done, sooner or later. The cost will be about forty thousand dollars."

"Then 'tis best when 'tis done quickly,'" Calman smiled as he recalled the famous line from *Macbeth*.

"There is something else, Calman. I need a new car."

"What's wrong with your present car?"

"I promised it to my younger son, Phillip."

"Won't this create some jealousy amongst the other children?"

"The two older children already have cars, and the others are too young."

"What will a new car cost?"

"Forty-five thousand."

"Why do you have to buy them a new car? You can probably purchase a demonstrator, or a used car in good condition for a fraction of the cost of a new car."

"No! I want him to have a new car. But I'll shop for a cheaper model."

"OK," Calman said, resigned. He made some notes in the file, and then looked at his watch. "OK. Time is up."

"Oh, Calman," she said, "You sound like a psychiatrist."

Calman stood up.

"All right," she said, "I'm leaving. But I've brought you a gift. Let me bring it in."

Before Calman could reply, she breezed through the door, walked over to the receptionist, and retrieved the gift she had left with Audrey. It was the Charlie Chaplin cane that Calman had admired.

"What is this?" The surprised Calman asked with a mixture of annoyance and delight.

"When I was in your home, I noticed your cane collection. Your wife told me that cane collecting was a hobby of yours. I want this cane to be owned by someone who will get some pleasure from it."

"But, wasn't this your father's cane? How can you part from it?" he objected.

"All the more reason why I want it to be yours," she said, as she slid out of the office, and disappeared rapidly down the hall.

CHAPTER XXXVI

Calman brought the cane home with him, and, entering the house performed a duck walk, twirling the cane. Ruth laughed. "My, my! A regular Charlie Chaplin!" In the evening, they went out for a walk. Ruth held onto his left arm. In his right hand, he carried the new cane.

"I'm thinking of returning the cane to Carole Williston," he said softly.

"Why? Do you have some ambivalence about keeping the cane?"

"Yes! The cane is too personal a gift. It belonged to her father, who died before she, and her mother, immigrated to Canada. She was very much attached to her father, and I'm sure it recalls important memories from her past. It is wrong for her to give it to me, and even more wrong for me to accept it."

"But don't you think she has considered that?"

"No doubt she has."

"Hasn't she grown rather dependent on you? Doesn't she tell you her confidences, discuss her children with you; seek your advice, as she probably would have done with her father?"

"Yes, I think that is true."

"So, you're a father figure for her. The gift of the cane is a symbol, marking the transference of her reliance on her father to you. Surely you can see that."

"I see that…but maybe there is something more."

"You mean that she's infatuated with you," Ruth smiled. "Of course she is."

"Perhaps more…"

"You mean she's in love with you…"

"And that too!"

"It's part of the transference process. I think she needs you more than you realize, Dr. Freud. She's very vulnerable, and if you return the cane, she may perceive it as a rejection. Keep the cane."

CHAPTER XXXVII

January 1979! Ruth was due for another check-up at the Princess Margaret Hospital, and Calman accompanied her. This time, she underwent a grueling set of tests. While she was resting from the ordeal, Dr. Sutherland appeared, and beckoned Calman to follow him into his office, which was no larger than a cubicle. As they entered the small office.

"You know, my wife speaks about you with great affection," Calman said.

"Thank you! She's a wonderful lady."

"How's my wife doing doctor?" The doctor's brows furrowed:

"Sir, please take a seat," he offered, but Calman remained standing dreading what was to follow.

"I'm afraid she's not doing well. The cancer is spreading…" He started to describe the actions of white corpuscles over red, and continued with a litany of Latin and medical terms. The blood drained from Calman's face. He interrupted the doctor.

"But I thought she was improving."

"Not really. The chemo treatments she was taking helped delay the inevitable. But the cancer has now spread to the vital organs."

"Can you not give her larger doses of chemo?"

"I'm sorry. There's nothing more that we can do."

"How much?"

"How much?" the doctor repeated.

"How much time does Ruth have?" Dr. Sutherland turned his gaze to the floor.

"Six, perhaps, eight weeks. That's about all." Calman let out a sob, but quickly brought himself under control.

"Will she suffer?" He was shaken.

"She'll be heavily sedated. We'll give her morphine."

"Will she remain in the hospital?"

"We can do nothing more for her here. It is best that she be at home."

"Does she know?" Calman asked, his face ashen, his voice cracking.

"Your wife is very stoic. Yes, she knows." The strain was telling on the doctor too, as tears welled in his eyes. Calman pulled out a handkerchief to dry his eyes, and extended his hand to the doctor.

"Thank you! You have been very good to us during the past few years. You're a good man, and a kind man." He thought of the Baron's words – *tres simpatico.*

On the way home, Cal held her hand. She was, oh, so weary.

CHAPTER XXXVIII

April 18, 1979. Calman tiptoed into the bedroom. Ruth was resting quietly. "Who is it?" Somehow, though her organs were deteriorating rapidly, her auditory perceptions had grown keener, more acute. She had heard him enter the room. He bent over her, kissed her forehead, and whispered, "You have a visitor. It's an old friend from Philadelphia. Do you remember Renee?"

"Renee? Goodness me. It's been so long. Could you raise me up, Cal?" He put his arms around her and lifted very gently until she was sitting nearly upright. "Would you put a shawl around my shoulders?" He did as she requested. "Now please pass me the cosmetic bag." He handed her the bag. She painstakingly withdrew a lipstick tube, and applied it to her lips as Calman held up a hand mirror, and then dabbed some rouge on her cheeks.

"There, that's better, don't you think?" He smiled.

"Why, you never looked prettier."

"Now, you can let in Renee."

April 19, 1979! Calman again tiptoed into the bedroom to tell Ruth she had another visitor. But she was in a deep sleep, and he was unable to rouse her. In a panic, he called Dr. Harris, who lived two doors away. The doctor came over immediately. He was out of breath. He checked her breathing, then her pulse. He wrapped the blood pressure device around her arm. Her face was pallid. After a long interval the doctor announced, "She has entered a comatose state."

"What does that mean?" Calman asked painfully.

"I believe she will pass away very soon, probably tonight. The doctor could see that Cal was in great distress, and he placed his hand on Calman's shoulder, in an act of compassion. Then the doctor turned, and walked out of the room, and out of the house, with head bent.

The nurse entered the room and took Calman's hand. "Come," she said, "I've prepared a cup of tea for you, with a sandwich. You haven't had a morsel all day. You've got to eat something." Calman let her lead him towards the kitchen. "It's on the table," she said, nudging him forward. The nurse remained behind with Ruth.

Calman sat on the chair in the kitchen, and listened to the silence. The sandwich remained on the plate, untouched. Suddenly, he had a terrifying sensation. He walked swiftly to the bedroom where Ruth lay unmoving. The nurse was putting down the stethoscope. Calman saw her swollen eyes. "Oh sir," she wept, "she's gone."

CHAPTER XXXIX

For a week, Calman did not leave the house, but remained home, and mourned. The golden lab, Maximilian, sat beside him, resting his head on Calman's knee, looking at him with soulful eyes. Numerous visitors came to pay their respects. But Carole Williston was not one of them. However, he did receive a note of condolence from her. Then he received a letter from the Cancer Society informing him that Dr. Carole Williston had made a significant contribution to them in memory of Ruth.

Calman returned to work the following week, but was unable to concentrate. He kept the door closed for fear the staff would hear him erupting into sobbing spells. One of his partners, Fred Landers, walked in carrying a bottle of Walker's Black Label and two glasses. He saw Calman's red and swollen eyes, and pulled up a chair facing him. He poured a drink for himself, and then pushed the bottle, and the empty glass, towards Calman. Fred said nothing. He was waiting for Calman. Finally Calman poured himself a drink. There was no clinking of glasses. They drank in silence. When, at last, Calman found his voice, he addressed his friend.

"Tell me, what is the most important thing in the world to you?" He expected Fred to say, "my family," or "my health," because Fred's health was precarious. Twice, he had been to Cleveland for open-heart surgery. But, instead, after thoughtful consideration, Fred answered, "I guess it would have to be my relationship with people." Calman knew at once that his wise friend was giving him a message, a signal that he was there for him.

"Perhaps you should go away for a week or two," Fred offered sympathetically. "No," Calman replied miserably, "It's too soon."

He wanted to continue with his morning visits to the synagogue, where he joined others in prayer, something he had never done before. After morning prayers, he would drive down to the office. At the end of the first week, after his return, on Friday morning, Calman had a business appointment away from the office. His meeting took place at the Toronto Livestock Exchange, at the west end of the city, with his client, Gustav Masters. Gus owned a ring in the Exchange, and was kept very busy buying, selling and auctioneering cattle.

"I heard of your loss," said Gustav "Is there anything I can do?"

"Thank you Gus. Somehow life will go on."

"If you wish, we can put off this meeting for a couple of weeks."

"No! No! That's the last thing I want to do."

Gustav's secretary brought in coffee and doughnuts. As he was reaching to take a doughnut, Calman's eye caught site of a cane lying across Gustav's desk. It was an ordinary cane hewn from birch, but it had an elongate stem. Calman lifted the cane and inspected it.

"What is this cane?" he asked with curiosity. "Oh, all the cattle dealers have one. They use it to prod the cattle. It comes in very handy."

Calman now turned to business. "What's on your mind, Gus?"

"Well, you know James Sturgess, who works for me?"

"Sure! You're referring to Jimmie. He's a bright kid."

"He's one of the best cattle brokers in the country. And now he's planning to leave me. He wants to go into business for himself. And I can't afford to lose him."

"It takes a few bucks to buy out a ring. Does he have the money?"

"His uncle is willing to finance him, and his wife is pushing him to take the plunge. If he leaves, I'll not only lose my best man, but he'll take away half of my customers."

"I see. But doesn't he have to acquire a ring first?"

"That's right! There's half a ring available, which he has his mind set on buying. The old man, McPherson, is very ill, and he wants to sell."

"Why don't you pre-empt him? You've known old Mac for many years. And you've been close to him. Go up and see the old boy and make him an offer he can't refuse."

"But Jimmy will be mad."

Calman stopped him.

"Mad? So what! Whatever he knows about this business, he's learned from you. You're the one who should be mad. After you get control of the other ring, you can make him an offer."

"What should I offer him?"

"Let him buy a twenty-five percent interest in the company. So, he won't be beholden to his uncle. When he's paid up offer him another twenty-five percent."

When Calman returned to his office at noon, the receptionist, Audrey, informed him that he had just missed Dr. Williston.

"She came in to see you this morning. She waited more than two hours, but then had to return to her office. She was expecting several patients."

"Well, I didn't schedule an appointment with her for today. Did she say what she wanted?"

"I think she wanted to console you over the loss of your wife. She left something for you. I put it on your desk."

Calman walked into his office, and was startled to find a vase, simple but elegant, containing a cluster of forget-me-nots. He realized that Carole had culled these flowers herself from her garden. He was agitated, as he had been when she presented him with the cane, and he didn't know what to make of the offering. Was this intended as a prelude to some sort of courtship? If so, it was not only inappropriate, but also offensive to Calman. Or, was it simply an act of kindness? He decided not to respond to her until after the weekend.

CHAPTER XL

Sunday morning. Nine a.m. The doorbell rang, and Calman went to answer it. There stood Dr. Allan Sherman. Calman was surprised to see him, but was bolstered by his presence.

"Why doctor, it's good to see you. Come in please."

Allan stepped in. "I dropped by to see how you're getting along."

"I'm all right, I guess…as well as one might expect," he answered. "I was about to have some coffee. Will you join me"?

"Yes, I'd be glad to." Calman knew that Allan had been at the funeral, but that he had not come to pay his respects at the house of mourning. He was glad that he was here now. Ruth was an enigmatic woman, and Calman had a great and urgent need to discover everything about her that he did not already know. They sat in the library, and the housekeeper served them coffee, and bagels. Calman started to talk:

"You know doctor…"

Allan interrupted him.

"As you know, Ruth and I were very good friends. She always called me Allan. So you should call me Allan, too."

"Thank you. I will. I was going to say that Ruth admired you."

"Well, I admired her, too. She was unique, one of a kind."

"In what way did you find her unique?" Calman asked.

"She was an exceptional person in several ways. Firstly, she was a natural wit."

"Yes, she could really coin a phrase. Sometimes, she would emphasize a point with a humorous Yiddish expression. You know, she spoke Yiddish fluently."

"I know that," said Allan. "She could also express herself well in English."

"She was articulate. Her thoughts were always stated with a kind of eloquent precision."

"Cal, why don't you share with me some of your memories of Ruth?" Calman realized that Allan was deliberately leading him, that this was a healing process, and he welcomed the opportunity to talk about Ruth.

"Yes, she was an insatiable reader. There was always a book at her bedside. When she was a girl, she tried to memorize the dictionary. As a child of eight, she could name, and identify, all the prehistoric animals. Do you know what she was reading before she began to slip away? Maimonides' *"Guide for the Perplexed."*

"But she never lost her humour or her light touch," the doctor observed. Calman could not get enough.

"Tell me more of the special qualities you saw in her."

"She was an excellent counsellor. She had great insight, and she knew how to draw people out, to make them discover themselves."

"Yes, and she was an admirer of Socrates."

The telephone rang, and Calman lifted the receiver.

"May I speak to Mr. Calman Mencher?" said the strained male voice. "Yes, this is he," Calman replied. The voice continued, hesitating.

The Chaplin Cane

"I don't know if you remember me. My name is Kenneth…Kenneth Hughes. I am Carole Williston's former husband." Calman was both baffled, and annoyed, by this strange call.

"Yes, Ken, I remember you," he said impatiently, wondering what sort of prank the man was up to. Calman wanted to get back to his guest, but the man seemed distraught, so Calman let him continue.

"Carole was on her way to visit her mother in Orangeville, on Friday. The car, which she was driving, swerved and went out of control on the highway, and was involved in an accident." There was a long pause, and Calman thought he detected a sob. He waited with trepidation. "She was killed instantly."

"Ohh! Ohh!" was all Calman could utter." Allan came towards him in alarm. "Th….thank you for letting me know." His voice was very low. Returning the phone to its cradle, he sank back into the chair.

"What has happened, man…for God's sake?" Allan demanded.

"Something terrible," his voice cracked. "No, it's a trick. It can't be true. I must be hallucinating. It's a nightmare."

Allan noticed a bottle of brandy in the liquor cabinet. He poured two stiff shots and handed one to Calman.

"Here, drink this down," Allan ordered. Calman downed his brandy with one gulp. "Now tell me what happened," Allan repeated.

Calman recounted to him his relationship with Carole Williston starting from the day she first called, when he was pondering the mysteries of life in his office above Charlie Tepper's law firm.

"All right," Allan ordered him, "Now, call Dr. Williston's home and verify what this Ken fellow told you." Cal looked up the number in the phone directory, his hands shaking, and dialled the number. Carole's son, Paul, came to the phone.

"It's true," he wept. "Mother was killed in a car accident. She was at the wheel, and was accompanied by a medical colleague, Frank…I think you met him…who was in the passenger seat. Suddenly the car went out of control. It rolled over three times. Mother was decapitated. Frank survived with only a few minor scratches."

Calman shuddered.

"She was buried yesterday."

Monday! Calman was not a religious man, but according to Jewish tradition, Calman and his son went to the synagogue early each morning – seven a.m. – to recite the morning prayers, a daily ritual which continues for thirty days after the death of a family member, called the 'shloshim'. They ran into the rabbi of the synagogue, Rabbi Gershom Frieberg, who had officiated at Ruth's funeral. They shook hands.

"Calman," said the rabbi with some consternation, "You look terrible. You mustn't let Ruth's passing undermine your health. You know, she would not have wanted that. He led them into his private office. Books were piled up everywhere – on shelves, on his desk, on the chairs, on the floor. He moved some of the books off two chairs, and bade them be seated. He then sat down in his own chair behind the desk, and lacing his fingers together, and asked, "So what's the matter?"

Calman narrated the story of Carole to the rabbi as he had to Dr. Sherman. "So this friend of yours…"

Calman interrupted: "Client."

"All right! This client of yours, Dr. Williston, was a closet Jewess?"

"Yes, I suppose you could say that," Calman replied.

"Then you will go into the sanctuary now, and you will recite the kadish (the prayer for the dead) twice. The rabbi stood beside Calman and together they recited the mourner's words – *Yisgadal v'Yiskadash, shmai rabo…*

CHAPTER XLI

Wednesday! The receptionist ushered the two young people into Calman's office. They were Paul and Ellen, Carole's two eldest. Carole had drawn a codicil to her will after divorcing Ken, and had appointed Calman as her executor. The two had come to discuss the will. As it was nearly noon hour, Calman invited them to join him for lunch. They went to the restaurant across the street from his office, where he and Carole had once lunched. Calman ordered a glass of wine for each of them. Raising his glass he made a toast to Carole.

"To a gracious and lovely lady." They clinked glasses. Paul was the first of the young people to speak.

"Mr. Mencher, two weeks from today, there is going to be a memorial service for Mom. You meant a lot to her, and we would like you to be there."

"Of course, I'll come. Where will it be held, and at what time?"

"It will be held at Saint Michael's Anglican Church, and we were wondering if you would deliver the eulogy."

What would I say? He wondered to himself, *I've never delivered a eulogy…and in a church…* But without hesitation he said, "I would be honoured." Lunch was served. Paul again broke the silence.

"You know, Sir, Mother was very fond of you."

"Oh, come on," Ellen broke in. "Mom was in love with Mr. Mencher." She turned to Calman, "You know, I believe she always had a thing for you."

"Well anyway," Paul continued, ignoring his sister, "we knew that you had just lost your wife, and that you were distraught. Mother told us that she was a beautiful and intelligent person, and she greatly admired her. Still, we were hoping that someday, after you had recovered from your great loss, you would become a … a stepfather to us."

Ellen once again interjected, "Did you know that mother was Jewish?"

Calman smiled, ironically, as he recalled his last luncheon in the same restaurant with Carole.

CHAPTER XLII

Two weeks later, Calman entered the stately cathedral of Saint Mikes. He gazed up at the great vaulted ceiling, and caught his breath at the sheer magnitude of the chamber. He looked about, and saw the seats being filled. He watched as a young woman, and a young man, accompanied an old woman towards the front. She was dressed in black and wore a black veil. Though she leaned on a cane, she bore herself with dignity. He recognized Mrs. Waitzer, and assumed the two young people were Carole's younger children. Calman waited for the service to begin. Then he heard his name being called.

An usher led him to the pulpit. Standing before the lectern, he spoke without notes. His voice, ordinarily thin, resonated through the acoustic hall. He spoke of their first meeting twenty-eight years ago. He spoke of her father, and how she had pined for him. He mentioned her mother by name, and each of her five children. He said nothing of Ken. He concluded by a quote from the Roman poet, Catullus.

"We send with thee, unto eternity

Our love and our farewell."

Everyone was invited for lunch to Carole's home. It was a warm afternoon, and the sun shone brightly. Ellen came over to Calman, and kissed him on the cheek. She put her arm through his, and they strolled through the garden. She plucked a flower, and handed it to him. He looked at her quizzically.

"They're called forget-me-nots," she said, and they continued their sauntering. A tall, fat man, almost bald, wearing a white shirt, but no jacket, his potbelly protruding over his belt, approached them carrying a tray of pastries.

"I'm Kenneth Hughes," he said grinning. Calman did not recognize him. "Try one of these pastries. They're delicious."

"Thank you," said Calman, as he extended his hand to reach for one.

"No, not that one. Try the other one, the éclair."

Napoleon," Calman corrected him.

CPSIA information can be obtained at www.ICGtesting.com
Printed in the USA
LVOW11s0921281215

468074LV00002B/73/P